Gently Touch the Milkweed

Other Books by Lynn Hall

RIDE A WILD DREAM

THE SECRET OF STONEHOUSE

THE SHY ONES

TOO NEAR THE SUN

Gently Touch the Milkweed

Lynn Hall

JACKET PAINTING BY ROD RUTH

FOLLETT PUBLISHING COMPANY
CHICAGO

About the Author

Lynn Hall's interests are young people, dogs, and horses —in that order. She makes her living writing books for young readers, and her three main interests figure prominently in her stories. Her earlier books are: *The Shy Ones, The Secret of Stonehouse, Ride a Wild Dream,* and *Too Near the Sun.*

Miss Hall has lived in Denver, Ft. Worth, Louisville, Chicago, and Des Moines, and she has worked as a telephone operator, a veterinarian's assistant, a handler of show dogs, and an advertising copywriter. None of her varied activities, however, brought her complete satisfaction until she began to write a few years ago.

Miss Hall lives in the village of Garnavillo, in northeast Iowa. Between books, she reads or sketches or explores the nearby hills and woodlands with a dog or two at her heels.

ISBN 0-695-40143-2 Titan binding
ISBN 0-695-80143-0 Trade binding

Library of Congress Catalog Card Number: 71-118923

First Printing I

For my sisters,
Lois and Jan

Gently Touch
the
Milkweed

Chapter One

She was big-boned, more woman than child, with features too strong for her youth and skin reddened with the permanent chap of hard-water bathing. Her hair was tied back at her neck in a way that would have been appealing on a more delicately built head. There was no fat on her, but a suggestion of massiveness about her shoulders and hips.

Her dress, originally walnut brown, had lost much of its stain in the wash kettle; now it was more nearly silver-gray, except where the wet grass had darkened the hem. Down each side seam ran a red gingham insert, added nearly a year ago to allow her to breathe and remain decent.

She came slowly across the pasture, head down, eyes searching the grass. Every few steps, she bent to pick up a cow chip, twig, or sunflower stalk, and dropped it into

9

the white quilted sack that bumped across the hillocks in her wake. The sack had once been her petticoat. When she could no longer fasten it around her waist, it had been handed down to her older sister, Del. Now, with its waist sewed shut, it made a serviceable kindling sack, although it was beginning to lose some of its quilting here and there.

She whistled between her teeth as she walked. It was going to be a good day, she thought, sensing without really noticing the clarity of the sunup, the cool dryness of the air, the April texture of the grass against the soles of her feet—moist new shoots beneath last year's dead stalks. Mornings like this one made her want to stand and watch down the trail for the next wagonload of homesteaders passing through, made her notice the young men among them, especially those who traveled alone.

Suddenly buoyed by the freshness of the morning, she dropped her sack, flung her arms wide, and breathed a great deep breath. One gingham insert ripped, loudly, from armpit to waist. Sighing, she dropped her arms and moved on, enjoying the immodest touch of the breeze on her bare ribs when she stretched down for a twig.

After a few more steps she hoisted the sack and measured the weight of the kindling against the number there'd be at breakfast. "Seventeen of them," she mumbled, "plus the four of us." She frowned at the sack and went on filling it. As she turned to work back toward the house, she saw her father and one of their overnight lodgers standing among the covered wagons in the front yard. Her father's gestures were obvious. He was pointing out the mill across the trail, and the blacksmith shop, and where the town square was going to be. She shook her head and smiled.

Through the still morning came her mother's bellow. "Janet, get a move on. I need that kindling."

Heaving the sack over her shoulder and clamping her arm down over the gape in her dress, she strode across the field toward the house.

The main part of the house had been built five years ago, when she was twelve, but it was only now becoming old enough and familiar enough that she could look at it without seeing it. The east end was the original log cabin, squat and rough and almost windowless. Attached to the west end of the cabin and looming over it was the main house, which was now home, hotel, and eating place, while the cabin served as a general store. The newer section stretched for what seemed an incredible length along the road toward the river, with walls of rough-cut boards faded from gold to gray, their paintless surface marred by rust streaks from the nails. Rust streaks and all, it was the most impressive building in the county, so far.

When Janet came into the huge room that was kitchen, parlor, and public dining room, her mother was whipping the first batch of corn-dodger batter in a huge crock under her arm. The two of them were built in the same oversized scale, but there was a heaviness about the older woman that had nothing to do with physical weight. Her eyes were seldom fully opened, and her features seemed motionless even when she spoke. Vesta Borofen had the same prominent brow, nose, and chin as Janet, but they were tempered by maturity to form a handsome face, in spite of its lack of expression.

Janet passed behind her mother, slung down her pack in front of the stove, and began to chunk the kindling into the waiting firebox. When the fire was started, she dipped her hands briefly into the water reservoir at the back of the stove, and dried them with quick strops against her skirt.

"My dress tore again," she said.

Vesta turned to scowl at the exposed tear, then sighed and went back to her stirring. Janet pushed through the door that led to the family's bedrooms and came back a minute later in her other dress, a rusty green homespun.

There were noises overhead now—grunts, loud groaning yawns, rustling hay, and the stomping of feet into boots. Before the first batch of corn dodgers came off the stove, legs began descending the loft ladder against the wall. The men came down heavily, surefootedly; the women came cautiously, feeling for each rung and holding their skirts modestly against their legs.

Janet moved among the milling guests, carrying full tin plates from stove to table, smiling when someone smiled first, otherwise ignoring them. Her father was there now, talking to everyone, laughing his loud host-laugh, making his way slowly toward the head of the table. One arm rode casually on Will Junior's shoulders.

"You can sit down now," Janet said.

Those who heard her assembled around the table, and the rest followed, one by one. She started down toward the empty end of the table, where she usually sat, but her father's arm stopped her.

"Here. Sit here by me. I want you to meet these folks."

Obediently she stepped over the bench and sat, knocking the edge of the table with her knees on the way down. Her father was at the head of the table, Will Junior on his right, Janet on his left. Beside Will Junior sat the man Willard had been showing the settlement to, before breakfast. She looked at him and his family and braced herself for the introductions.

"This is my girl Janet. Janet, this's Mel Makinich and his good wife . . ."

"Mary Pat," the woman said. "Hello, Janet."

While Janet was registering a liking for the woman across the table, Willard went into his explanation of his daughter. ". . . oldest girl, Del, got married last year, married a young doctor down in Kansas territory. Janet here, she was the only boy I had for a lot of years, till Will Junior come along. Course, she ain't a boy anymore"—Janet flushed deeply and hated him—"but I'd still put her up against any of 'em with a rifle or a horse or a hard day's work."

Will Junior spoke through a mouthful of corn dodger. "I can shoot better than her any day, and yesterday I got her down and made her yell uncle. You should have seen me, Pa."

Willard beamed at his son and rumpled his hair.

"Tell me more about Willard's Ford, Mr. Borofen," the man across the table said.

"Call me Willard. No formalities in Willard's Ford. Well now, I'll give you the facts as they stand. The way I see it, this place has just naturally got to take off and grow like you've never seen a town grow. We got a good little river, a double mill, plenty of water just under the grass roots, and the best soil you ever turned. Plenty of timber along the river, plenty of open prairie that don't need clearing. Good trail east and west, and we're just sixty mile from Nebraska City and the Missouri River. Within the next year or two I figure to see this town get to be one of the biggest in the county. As a matter of fact, I've got a man coming out here any day now, from Illinois. Professional city planner, he is. With his know-how and Willard's Ford's natural assets, there's no telling how fast this place is going to grow."

Janet ceased to hear the chant she knew by heart. Without lifting her head, she took a closer look at the

14

Makiniches, on the off chance they would be the one family in a hundred or so who succumbed to Pa's selling and stayed to become neighbors.

They appeared to be in their early thirties. He was unusually tall, with salt-and-pepper hair and large regular features that were undermined by a softness around his jaw. His table manners were better than average, and he looked at Willard with keen-eyed intelligence. His wife was small beside him. Her face had a pleasant, childlike quality accented by freckles and the wiry untidiness of her auburn hair. She raised her eyes suddenly, caught Janet studying her, and returned the look with a quick grin, a half wink. Warmed and flustered, Janet got up and brought a fresh pitcher of molasses from the stove.

". . . matter of fact," Willard was saying, "there's a quarter right in this very section that can be bought at darn near government prices, and it's got a dandy cabin, a good well, and everything. It's behind me and just to the east. Fellow that homesteaded it took off for California in forty-nine and got killed out there. His kin live down by Corning. I know they been wanting to sell the place."

He paused to fill his mouth and let the idea sink in, then went on. "You'd be just half a mile from town, soon as the town gets built. You could set up your newspaper downtown here and live out there all year round easy as anything. And I'll venture to say that in a few years, when Willard's Ford begins spreading out, you can sell off building lots at pretty fancy prices."

The Makiniches exchanged uncertain looks.

"Tell you what," Willard said quickly. "I'll just take you folks over there after breakfast, and you can see what you think."

They looked at each other again. This time Mary Pat nodded.

When the dining room was cleared of people and the tin plates stacked precariously beside the dishwater kettle, Vesta said, "I'll do these up. You better get started on the beds."

Janet took the pitchfork from the wall beside the loft ladder and began to climb, holding the unwieldy fork in one hand and grabbing from rung to rung with the other.

The loft was divided across the middle by a wall of hanging quilts that separated the men's side from the women's. The beds that lined the walls in two rows were simple hay pallets. Willard had built them by setting broad planks on edge and nailing them to the floorboards, to hold in the hay. The beds were one plankwidth high, six feet long, and three feet wide.

Before she started on the beds, Janet flung back the partition quilts and opened the small windows at either end of the loft. While fresh air dispelled the odors of sweat and feet and sour breath, she took the pitchfork and began to make the beds. Where the hay level was lower than two-thirds, she added forkfuls of sweet prairie grass from the stack in the corner of the room. At the beds that still held plenty of hay, she just fluffed it up with the wooden tines of the fork, carefully burying any noticeable soiled spots.

At the east window she paused to look out. Directly below her, the sod of the cabin roof was dotted with purple and white clover and the small pink flowers Janet especially liked, although she didn't know their name. The grass of the sod was showing bright green this morning, through last year's leftover stalks.

Far to the left a movement caught her eye. She leaned out the window and craned to see through the trees. It was Pa and Will Junior, with the Makiniches, moving across the pasture toward the empty cabin that crouched out of sight beyond a low hill. The figures crested the hill, paused a few moments while Pa's arm pointed east and west, and then they disappeared from her view.

There were sixteen for lunch—the Makiniches and their two children, two families whose covered wagons and teams waited outside, and the four Borofens. While she handed out the plates, Janet listened to the conversation from Pa's end of the table. Her placid face hid the excitement she felt, knowing the Makiniches were going to stay.

". . . still plenty of time to get a corn crop in this

17

year," Willard was saying. "My boy'll give you a hand—Janet too, if you want her—and I know a man with a breaking plow and a crew that he hires out."

She filled her own plate and sat down near them. Mary Pat Makinich smiled broadly at her. When there was a break in the conversation, Janet caught Mr. Makinich's glance. "Are you really going to start a newspaper here?"

His eyes kindled, warming her. "You bet I am. I've got my press right out there in the wagon, all bought and paid for. All I've been needing was the right up-and-coming young town to settle in, and I must say Willard's Ford seems to have what I was looking for."

"I don't mean to rush you," Willard said, "but if your mind's made up, we can go down to Corning after dinner and close the deal. We'll take my spring buggy."

Mel nodded. "Maybe your wife would like to go along for the ride," he said, glancing toward Vesta at the stove.

"Nah. She don't care about buggy riding. Will Junior'll want to go, and that'll about fill up the wagon."

"How about me?" Janet heard herself say. "I'd like to go along once." But she knew the answer before her father spoke.

"You better stick around and keep an eye on the store, with Will Junior gone. And your ma'll be needing you to help with supper. We won't be back till late."

When the dinner mess in the kitchen was finally cleared away, the house took on its afternoon quiet.

18

Vesta settled near the stove with a pan and a pile of corn ears to be shelled, and Janet climbed the ladder to the loft. She idled along the rows of beds, stopped to pull a splinter from the ball of her foot, went on to the east window, and eased herself through it.

"Careful there, lady," she muttered as she lowered herself to the cabin roof. Straddling the ridgepole, she walked on hands and feet to the outer edge of the roof. To anyone watching from the window behind her, she would have presented an awkward picture. Although the sod roof was in the shade now, the earth felt warm to her touch. She eased down the trail-side slope of the roof, then lay back against it. Her feet, crossed at the ankles in premeditated femininity, hung over the edge of the roof, while her head rested on the ridge.

From the angle at which she was canted, she could stare at the sky, watch the trail in both directions, or spy on the action at the mill, across the trail and through the trees. She could make out three or four wagons over there, waiting for their grain to be milled. From that direction came the intermittant chink of a horseshoe game and the high-pitched voices of shouting boys.

Maybe I'll go over there after while, she thought. But first she needed some time alone to resent being excluded from the drive to Corning. Her resentment was stronger than usual, and it centered around the fact that she was now an insignificant household drudge, classified with Ma, in the eyes of the Makinich family.

A figure appeared on the trail and became Charlie

Gates, the blacksmith. He turned into the yard and stopped just beneath her dangling feet, at the cabin door. His rough hand closed around one ankle, but she kicked him away.

"Don't, Charlie. I'll come down there and clean you out."

He laughed and went on inside. Janet heard him call through the empty cabin-store, heard Ma lumbering across the long dining room toward him.

A few minutes later Vesta shouted, "Janet. Customer."

Janet groaned. Oh, why can't you wait on somebody, just once. It's not a bit hard. Aloud, she called, "I'm coming." Wearily she rolled over onto her stomach, slid down over the lip of the roof, and dropped to the ground.

In the dimness of the cabin Charlie said, "Gimme a half pound of number eights, will you?"

She moved around the crates and barrels and dress-goods bolts, stepped over the pile of harness in the corner, and reached to the top shelf for the box of horseshoe nails. She poured a stream of square-headed number eights into Charlie's handkerchief, hefted it, added a few more nails, and handed him the packet.

"Your pa owed me fifty cents on that set of ox shoes I did for him last week. Take these off of that, will you?" Charlie said.

She nodded and made a note. Then came their ritual. Today her heart wasn't in it.

"When you goin' to marry me, Janet?"

She answered with a quick punch in the vest area of his stomach, and he countered by twisting her arm up hard behind her back. Because Charlie's stupid game irritated her today, she put more force than usual into her punch and resisted his arm-twisting with genuine defiance.

"Come on, Charlie, you're breaking my arm."

Immediately he let go. He seemed confused by her tone, and she regretted her snappishness. By way of a peace offering, she said, "Did you hear we're getting some neighbors?" She hoisted herself to a seat on the counter and began to describe the Makiniches.

Chapter Two

"All right, kids, scoot on outside and run off some of that wildness."

With a wave of her hand Mary Pat excused the children from the lunch table. Then she and Mel settled back in their chairs, full and content and in no special hurry. In the quiet of the cabin each followed his own ambling thoughts. After a while, Mary Pat picked up the conversation interrupted during lunch by the children's chatter.

"I don't think she's really unfriendly. I get the feeling she likes us all right."

"Vesta?"

"Mmm. I think she just doesn't like to leave her kitchen. Six days we've been out here now, and any other woman would have been over to visit half a dozen times already, if only to see what I'd done to the cabin. Still, like I say, she's pleasant enough when we go over there, so it doesn't really bother me."

Mel tipped his chair back against the wall and fished a packet of cigarette papers from his shirt pocket. Slowly, savoring the anticipation of this after-dinner smoke, he tapped the tobacco from its sack into the shallow trough of paper, ran his tongue along one edge, and rolled the cylinder up tight.

Picking a shred of tobacco from his tongue, he said, "You know which one I like best of that whole family?"

She shook her head.

"Janet."

Mary Pat grinned. "She is a good kid. It's a shame she's such a cow. But it's kind of fun having her around. She reminds me of a big puppy, falling all over itself for a pat on the head."

"Janet is one of those cases of still waters running deep, though. Take a look at that head sometime. It's kind of—"

"Still waters?" Mary Pat laughed. "That girl has a voice like a bull moose."

Mel smiled at the aptness of the comparison, but argued, "No, now, be serious. Did I ever tell you about my theory about—"

"Oh, you and your theories." She rose and brought the huge crockery washbowl to the table. While they talked, they went automatically through the routine; Mel whittled shavings from the soap chunk into the crock on the table, while Mary Pat poured in boiling water from the stove and cold water from the bucket by the door. She began washing the dishes, and he settled back in his chair with his feet on the table but carefully out of her way. To the sloshing of the water, he elaborated on his theory about people like Janet Borofen.

"You should have been a philosopher," she said, with an air of having said it countless times.

"No money in it." He closed his eyes to savor the last bittersweet pull on his cigarette. His mind drifted with the smoke for a few minutes. Then he came back to finish his argument.

"I still say that girl has a side to her nature that's just as thin-skinned and sensitive as anybody."

Mary Pat carried the crock to the open door of the cabin and pitched the water out. "Here comes old Thin-skin now," she said. "At a dead gallop."

She ran hard, clenched fists pumping, feet jarring the ground. Her mouth was open, smiling, her eyes half-shut against the wind. Her lungs began to ache, but she was so full of tingling life that she didn't slow down till the cabin was in sight. Then, panting, she stopped to re-tie the ribbon that held back her hair. She walked on slowly, hoping the breeze would dry her perspiration before she got to the Mackiniches'.

Mel was coming out the door as she approached. "Halloo there, neighbor," he called.

She answered, breathlessly, and came up beside him. For an instant she stood looking up at him, basking in his bigness, his open-faced acceptance of her.

"Come on around back and see my new cornfield."

Together they turned and walked around the cabin toward the strip of black fresh-broken sod that contrasted sharply with the pastel grass. The breaking crew had just finished their lunch and were starting back to work. Mel and Janet stood at the edge of the plowed strip and watched.

Six yoke of oxen threw their weight against the drag of the massive breaking plow. The plow had two blades, one behind the other, attached to an oak beam six feet long and heavier than a large man. While the plow-owner's young son walked beside the two lead oxen, guiding them with his switch, two men rode astride the plow's beam to force it down, and another man fought the lurching handle. Across the ground they moved, slowly, fighting the ages-old mats of grass root that bound the soil.

"How much are you going to break?" Janet asked.

"Ten acres. They've been averaging two acres a day and charging me six dollars a day for it, so ten's about all I can afford this year." They were quiet a while; then he went on. "Maybe by next year I'll be so busy with the newspaper I won't want to work more than ten acres of corn, anyhow."

It excited Janet to think about Mel as an editor of a

newspaper. For the first time in all her years of listening to her father air his dreams for Willard's Ford, she began to feel a personal interest in the settlement becoming a full-fledged town, big enough to support a newspaper. During the past six days, the attraction she felt to the Makinich family had begun to take on substance—an afternoon of hoeing beside Mary Pat in the garden plot, a family joke they shared with her, a pat on the arm from Mel as he passed. It became important to her that they like Willard's Ford, that they stay here.

"I guess I'd better go help the men," Mel said finally. "Why don't you go keep Mary Pat company?"

In the cabin she found Mary Pat just settling herself down to a lap full of sewing. Her chair was barely inside the cabin door, in the stream of sunlight that brightened the rough puncheon floor and illuminated the colors in the rag rug. Janet sat on the doorsill beside Mary Pat's chair.

"What are you making now?" she asked, squinting up at the red cotton she herself had sold Mary Pat.

"Curtains for the bedroom window. See, this red matches the red in the quilt."

As Janet's gaze wandered around the big main room of the cabin behind her, she saw the same bright red reflected in the gingham of the curtains, in the geranium on the window ledge, in the rag rug and the crazy quilt on the children's bed in the far corner, in the embroidered mottoes on the wall, and in the glints of sun in Mary Pat's hair.

26

"You like red a lot, don't you?" Janet said.

"Mmm."

Warmed by the sun in her face, lulled by the all but imperceptible sounds of thread pulling through cloth, of her friend breathing, Janet relaxed against the door frame and acknowledged that she was happy. From behind the cabin came the shrill voices of the children and the muted sounds of creaking ox yokes and shouting men.

"You're awful quiet today," Mary Pat muttered as she bit off her thread. "Finish telling me about all the families around here. You were telling me about the Crows yesterday, I think. Now that's the ones on the other side of the river, right? How many children do they have?"

By the time she left the cabin and started home, the afternoon had a feeling of lateness. Shadows were beginning to move out across the grass from the line of trees that bordered the river. Her long, loose stride ate up the path.

It was a new path. It had just become noticeable within the last day or two, a line of flattened grass that ran from the Makinich cabin almost straight southwest across the gentle swells of open prairie. Behind Willard's Ford the path met the edge of the river timber. It became indefinable under the trees, but appeared again at the edge of the Borofens' clearing, near the outhouse.

The outhouse was one of her father's chief sources of pride. To own one at all, in Adams County in 1857, was a mark of superiority, and this one was a dandy, with separate sides for men and women and lath screens modestly shielding the doors.

Janet walked swiftly toward home. The aura of Mary Pat and Mel stayed with her and lightened her, although she couldn't have pinned down exactly what quality about the family woke this warm response in her.

As she rounded the outhouse, she saw Pa standing beside a buggy out near the trail. He was helping unhitch the horse while he talked to the owner with animation Janet could see from the backyard. Immediately, the man aroused her curiosity; he was wearing a business suit.

He was a small man, erect and self-contained and highly polished. As she approached, she saw his neatly carved face, the geometric waves of black and silver hair. When she reached the men and stood beside Pa, the little man's cologne met her and made her want to back away. The man glanced at her but went on talking in a musical, wide-range voice, as though she weren't there.

". . . a sleeping giant. A sleeping giant, Mr. B, and I intend to put a burr under its tail. Now you're sure the half section directly across from the blacksmith shop is still government land? Because that's the place for the town square. We'll get over to the land office first thing and file a township claim on that piece—"

Willard interrupted. "This's my girl Janet. Janet, this's Mr. Jay Zupin, from Illinois. He's the city planner I wrote to. He thinks—"

"Delighted, delighted," the man sang, without looking toward her. "You're going to be a wealthy man, Mr. B. Before you know it, I'll have people swarming into this town, and you'll be selling off commercial lots along this road all the way from your barn to the river. Of course, we'll have to come up with a name that's got some class."

Janet glanced at Pa. His face was darkening, setting itself into hard planes. "Oh no, Zupin. There's one thing I got to insist on. I found this place, and it's going to be named after me. That's been my main idea all this—"

"Well, well, we won't argue that point for now. A minor matter. Shall we go inside and see about supper?"

Still ignoring Janet, Mr. Zupin turned toward the house, sweeping Willard along with him. Willard threw a questioning glance from Janet to the horse, which had yet to be unhitched. Glumly, she nodded and went to work on the girth buckles.

"That's some owner you got there," she muttered, giving the horse a friendly whack on the chest. When she looked back over her shoulder, the two men were disappearing through the cabin door. Mr. Zupin was leading the way, opening the door with the flourish of a host.

The evening of his second day under the Borofen roof, Mr. Zupin called a town meeting. In the afternoon he commandeered Will Junior and Janet to make the rounds of all the settlers within riding distance and spread the word. By suppertime they began to arrive, and by meeting time all seven homesteading families were there. Charlie the blacksmith came down the trail in clean overalls and his town shoes, ready to enjoy the meeting and to roughhouse with Janet if the opportunity came. Across the trail Carl Morton locked the mill and his one-room cabin, and came out from under his trees to join the doings. From the path beyond the outhouse came Mel and Mary Pat, with the little Makiniches racing in circles around them.

The two long tables had been pushed back against the walls of the dining room, and the four benches arranged in rows, facing the fireplace. While Willard and Mr. Zupin greeted the new arrivals at the cabin door and ushered them through the store into the dining room, Janet moved along the walls from lamp to lamp, lighting them against the deepening twilight. She raised her arms cautiously at each lamp, wary of the repaired seams of the gingham inserts under her arms. Will Junior was outside helping with the teams, and Vesta sat in her chair between the fireplace and the cookstove, talking to those who came near her but looking as though she did not intend to move from her chair. Her hands busied themselves with an embroidery hoop that held a square of quilting.

The back door, beside the loft ladder, opened to admit Charlie and Willard, who hefted between them the wheelless body of a small wagon. Jay Zupin followed close behind.

"Up here, men," he directed. "In front of the fire. Turn it over now, that's the spirit. There, that's fine."

He stood on the upside-down wagon box, which was now evidently a speaker's platform, and bounced a few times on the balls of his feet. As he did so, the chattering died down, and people worked themselves into the rows of benches. Janet moved to the back of the room and sat on the far end of a table. A few of the men preferred leaning against the tables or walls to the more total commitment of sitting on the low benches, which were well filled with women and children anyway.

Mel half-stood, half-sat against Janet's table at the opposite end near the speaker, one leg up, arms across his chest, his shoulders turned away from her. Mary Pat and the children sat near him on the front bench.

Twenty-two people, Janet counted silently, plus at least that many kids, not counting me. She didn't concern herself with which category she belonged to. It's almost like it was a town already.

The chill that went through her as she watched Jay Zupin step up onto the platform was part anticipation of what was about to happen to her life, and part dread of the unknown. A smaller, sour part of the chill was jealousy. Things were going to happen now, people were going to come, and there would be distractions for Mel and Mary Pat, more interesting things for them to do than to talk to old Janet.

The figure on the wagon box cleared his throat, and the last of the whispers ceased.

"Ladies and gentlemen, you are at this moment witnessing the birth of a city." He paused, eloquently. "I am Jay Arthur Zupin—that's J-A-Y, Jay, not the initial—and I am by profession a city planning director. When Mr. Borofen wrote to me, describing your fair—village—and asking for my professional assistance, I knew this place must be my next project. And let me say that I have never before seen a town site that showed such natural promise. Natural promise and a good beginning, thanks to Mr. Borofen, here.

"We must begin by forming a town company, a corporation, with officers and regular meetings. We will sell shares of stock in the company to enterprising investors back east, and use part of the profits to pay for the expenses of promoting our new city. My fee as City Planning Director will come from this fund, along with advertising costs, and I also recommend we hire an agent to meet the boats bringing settlers to Nebraska City; he'll tell the people the advantages of coming to live here. For the election of officers . . ."

As the room grew darker, the little man became more sharply outlined by the halo of the fire behind him. It shone through his hair, exaggerating its thick waves. It showed red through his ears and lay like gold on the shoulders of his suit. The fact that his features all but disappeared in the shadows only made his voice more hypnotic.

". . . half section just east of Mr. Morton for a

township claim, and I've been assured we'll have no difficulty there. We'll want a town square, with room in the center for the courthouse. Yes, good friends, the courthouse. I see no reason why our city shouldn't one day win the county seatship away from Corning. Our location, our natural resources . . ."

Jay Zupin cast a tall and broadening shadow from his platform to the front row of listeners. They sat utterly still, their faces turned up toward him, reflecting the light of the fire. In the dark corner behind the speaker, all that could be seen of Vesta Borofen was her dress, where the folds falling from her knees were outlined by firelight. The rest of her was in darkness, but her embroidery needle glinted steadily throughout the speech.

"I am calling on each one of you in this room tonight, every man jack, every good wife and tiny child, to pledge your utmost to our wonderful cause, the building of our city."

Applause, and from the men along the tables, loud syllables of agreement.

"Now I'm going to be a little more specific. I want all of you who have kin or friends or acquaintances back east to write to them immediately, and tell them to spread the word of the advantages our city offers to settlers. I want you, Willard Borofen"—Jay pointed dramatically—"to see to it that no travelers passing through here leave your hearth and home without being told why they should settle here instead of the barren wastelands of Nebraska or wherever they think they want to go.

"You, Charles Gates"—he stabbed at Charlie, startling him—"you must remodel your shop, build a high plank front on it, maybe go into the livery stable business if you're so inclined. Carl Morton, I want you to . . ."

And so it went. Willard found himself promising to enlarge his store, to turn over his lodging business to the couple from I¹linois whom Jay would bring here to build a genuine hotel. Mel Makinich agreed without hesitation that his newspaper should go into print at once, never mind about the corn crop.

When the obligations were all assigned, Jay's voice became lighter. "I can't tell you good people how gratified I am at your response. Gratified and proud to be one of you. Now just one more item before we adjourn this first monthly town meeting," he caroled, "but it's a very important item. I would like to propose that we call our new metropolis—Eden City!"

In the silence all faces turned to Willard. Janet felt the jarring of the table beneath as her father pushed away from it. He took a step toward Jay and bellowed, "No, by God. I'll give up my hotel business, I'll enlarge my store, I'll stand on my head, but I'll be da—*hanged* if I'll let anybody change the name of this town. It's always been Willard's Ford, and until they pitch the dirt on my coffin it's going to stay Willard's Ford. I was here first!"

34

Although Janet flushed at the childishness of his plea, she felt, and understood, the intensity behind it. To have a town named after you—that was something big, something bigger than any of their uncles or cousins could brag about. Pa wasn't going to give up Willard's Ford, at least not without a fight.

"I don't know," one of the women mused. "It has a kind of ring, don't it? Eden City. Eden City, Iowa."

A man answered from the dim far side of the room. "I'm with Willard. Nothin' wrong with the name Willard's Ford."

Skirts rustled as women turned on their benches to follow the volley of words. The argument brought relief from the tension of Zupin's hypnotism.

"We got to have a name with style, like Eden City."

"Why, nobody'd know what you was talking about. Eden City."

"There's a lot worse names than Willard's Ford."

Hilarity threatened the meeting as the men began calling out peculiar town names they had heard.

Above the din Jay's voice rose to command and quell. "All right, folks. We can decide this at the next meeting. You think it over between now and then. I want to thank you all for your splendid cooperation, and good night."

For nearly two hours after the adjournment, the room was alive with moving, chattering clusters of people. From group to group Willard and Jay moved, exchanging names and handshakes and enthusiastic compliments. The screams and whoops of liberated youngsters came in the open door from the black night outside.

Throughout the socializing Janet kept her perch on the dark end of the table. She swung her legs and followed with her eyes first one, then another, of the milling figures. She watched Pa as he beamed from Jay Zupin to Bill Crow. Even across the shadowy room she could feel the excitement he radiated. Not since the night Will Junior was born had she seen such animation in his face.

Then Mel crossed her vision and her eyes followed him. He seemed to be introducing himself around, telling people about his unborn newspaper, and at the same time keeping track of Mary Pat, who had settled happily with a nest of ladies in the middle of the room. Suddenly Mel was beside Janet's knee.

"What do you think about all this, Janny? Kind of exciting, isn't it, being in on the start of a city?"

She looked at him and wanted to say something quick and bright that would make him laugh. "I can't see that anything's been started, except a lot of talk. Ain't any more population here now than there was yesterday, except Mr. Zupin."

She was beginning to flush at the dumb hardness of her words when his eyes met hers and kindled. He laughed. "If I had a drink in my hand, I'd toast you. That's the soundest sense I've heard all evening. Well, I expect my tribe's about ready to head for home. Come on over tomorrow if you get time."

The room began to empty after that. Children were gathered and sorted; wagons creaked off into the night. A few of the families who lived some distance away accepted Willard's offer of the loft.

"No charge, of course," he said, smiling. "Just don't let on to the paying customers."

Vesta rose from her corner and folded away her embroidery. Janet went wearily into her room.

It was a windowless, sterile compartment almost completely filled by the hay bed along one wall. A narrow walkway went between the bed and the other wall, which was lined with clothes pegs. At the end of the walkway there was just room between the bed and the pegged wall for the wooden chest that held her belongings: her slate and rag, unused since the end of her schooling two years ago; the crude horse that Charlie had forged for her, long ago, out of worn ox shoes and number eight nails; her other shift and petticoat; her beaver-bristle hairbrush; three letters from a man in Colorado Territory who had proposed to her last year as he was passing through Willard's Ford. In the deepest corner of the chest was a ring made of human hair, braided and mounted on a narrow silver backing. It had belonged to her father's mother and had come to Janet because her disinterest in it was slightly less than Willard's and Del's had been, It never occurred to her to wear it, but she was rather fascinated by the delicacy of the braiding, and its presence enhanced the trunkful of possessions.

The unpainted plank walls were decorated on one side by her three other dresses—the green homespun and two equally faded winter linsey-woolseys. The wall behind the bed was covered by a patchwork quilt of predominant greens and browns, nailed up there to protect her from the peering eyes of Will Junior in the next room. The partition's cottonwood planks had been put up unseasoned and were badly warped and curling, leaving ample cracks for a peeking brother to see through.

She blew out her lantern and set it, smoking, on the trunk. Aimlessly her hands unbuttoned her dress and flung it through the dark toward its peg. With a sigh, she rolled down onto the bed. Again tonight, as she had every night since Del's wedding, she wished Del were here to talk to and then, in the next moment, blessed Del's absence, which allowed her to spread out as wide as she wanted across the bed. Sleep drifted in and numbed her.

"What do you think about all this, Janny. . . . If I had a drink in my hand, I'd toast you. . . . Janny . . ." Funny how much softer *Janny* sounded than *Janet*.

Chapter Three

The ten plowed acres of Mel's cornfield lay on the pale green folds of the prairie like a black patch. It was the only cultivated land in sight from Janet's vantage point atop the low hill south of the cabin. Against the upturned black earth, a line of figures moved slowly. Janet skirted the cabin and made her way across the furrows toward the workers. Twice her foot caught in the ropy tangle of exposed roots that lay on the ground's surface, and she fell.

As she neared the figures, she saw that they were, as she'd assumed, Mary Pat and the children, measuring off the corn hills. Mary Pat took a long step, poked a hole in the earth between her feet with a cottonwood branch, and stepped again. Behind her, eight-year-old Muffin squatted to drop five carefully counted seeds into each hole, while behind Muffin, five-year-old Jason, earnest and incredibly dirty, caved in the sides of the holes and pounded them with his fists until they disappeared. Several yards behind Jason, a pair of crows worked at digging the kernels up again. As she dropped her seeds, Muffin chanted, "Two to grow, two for the crow, and one to throw away."

Mary Pat stopped measuring when she saw Janet. "Hello," she called. "Isn't this a beautiful afternoon? The breaking crew finished up this morning, so the kids and I thought we'd start in with the planting. Two hours ago Mel said he'd be right out to take over for us, but he's all worked up about the newspaper after that speech of Mr. Zupin's last night. He's in the house, working on his first edition. You got dirt on your dress there."

Janet swatted some of the earth off the front of her dress and said, "Thanks. Want any help?"

"Well, I don't know. Looks like everything's taken care of. I've got a couple of good little helpers, here." Muffin and Jason beamed up at Janet. "But why don't you stay awhile and keep us company? Hey, you darn crows, stop that." Mary Pat threw a clod of earth at the birds, and the children ran toward them, flapping their arms and screeching. The crows circled and waited, just out of reach.

For a while Janet ambled along beside Mary Pat, basking in the woman's bright chatter and tossing an occasional clod at the crows. Then she left the planting crew and picked her way back across the field toward the cabin. She found Mel in his editorial office in the corner of the cabin's main room.

His sanctum was walled off from the rest of the room by the printing press and a desk made of three packing crates. The press resembled a small golden-oak table about four feet long and half as wide, with a metal cylinder the size of a small churn lying across the top. Inside the blocked-off corner were bundles of paper, a flat wooden box of type, and a small crate marked "Ink."

Mel sat in a cracked-leather chair that dominated the makeshift office. The top of his desk held a scattering of scribbled papers. He looked up from them when Janet entered the cabin.

"Do you want to be left alone?" she called.

"Come in, come in. Glad to see you. No, I can't concentrate anyway. Pull up a chair. I thought I'd get out a first issue right away—you know, an introductory sort of thing. I may have your brother deliver it around the county. Of course, I know it's not going to bring in any money for a long time, till we get some advertisers. But after last night I couldn't wait to get started. Here now, what do you think about these?" He leaned back in his chair and held at arm's length the sheet of paper he'd been doodling on.

He cleared his throat and pronounced, "The Willard's Ford Clarion, The Eden City Clarion, or The

Adams County Clarion. Or, the Willard's Ford Monitor? Or, I was thinking about The Free Press, or possibly The Tribune. Which do you like?"

Janet looked at his face, across the desk and beyond the expanse of his shirt front as he leaned back in his chair. His bright expectancy blanked her mind.

"Well? Which one do you like, Janny? Or don't you like any of them?"

"Read them again." He did, and this time she concentrated on what he was saying, rather than on the lovely important ring to his voice.

"I think maybe The Adams County Clarion," she said finally. "That has a nice sound to it."

He stabbed his pen in her direction. "I believe you're right. That way, we avoid any arguments about Willard's Ford versus Eden City." With a heavy flourish, he circled the name on the paper and scratched through the rejects. "You know, a newspaper can be an important force for the good of its community, and that's what I want this one to be, Janny. I used to dream about it back in Muscatine, working on the paper back there—a brand-new town, with my newspaper right there at its beginning, building that town in the right direction. Do you know what people out here need, more than any other one thing?" He leveled his eyes on her.

She was about to say "Cornmeal and fuel in winter" when he went on. "What they need more than anything is a sense of beauty. If you could see some of the rest of the world, you'd realize how much natural beauty there is here." He swept his arms in an embrace of Adams County. "But people are so busy scratching for a living they don't even look."

He leaned toward her across the littered desk top, and his voice fell to a level of quiet sincerity. "I think that's why I liked you right away. You might not seem like it to other people, but I understand human nature pretty well, being a newspaperman, and I think you have —sensitivity. For instance, when you came in just now, you were sensitive to the fact that I might want to be left alone."

Sensitivity. The word sang through her and struck a responsive nerve hidden deep under the hoyden exterior. Sensitivity. She cherished the word, knowing he'd retract it when he knew her better. She hunched deeper in the chair, stretching her legs and making her feet go pigeon-toed against the rough boards of the floor. But then the sinewy, dirt-rimmed feet looked preposterously ugly. She drew them back under the chair.

He was talking on about the paper. "I'm going to run at least one poem in each issue, not fancy poems no one would understand, but the down-to-earth kind, about everyday life and sunsets and things like that, so people might possibly start appreciating their surroundings more. And I was thinking about a debating society—"

He broke off. Through the open door they saw Jay Zupin's buggy lurching over the hill. It tossed and jarred across the rough ground, although the horse was only jogging.

When he came inside, Jay filled the cabin with his briskness. He passed Janet and grasped Mel's hand across the desk. "There's the editor, already at work on our newspaper. Crude surroundings don't mean a thing in this business, right?"

Mary Pat and the children came in then, drawn by the sight of the buggy outside. Mary Pat wiped her hands on her dress and, smiling, accepted Jay's half-bow.

"There she is, and how are you this lovely day, Miz . . ." His face went blank as he sought the name.

"Makinich," she said, grinning. "Like 'mackinaw that itches'. It's a hard one to remember. Can I get you some coffee? Janet, coffee?"

Janet shook her head, but Jay accepted, then dismissed Mary Pat with a turn of his shoulder. He took the chair she offered—the only other chair in the cabin—and swung it close to Mel's desk.

"Mr. M, you and I have got to have a serious talk." His manner excluded the women. As Janet got up and began edging uncomfortably toward the door, Mary Pat caught her attention. The little woman rolled her eyes at Jay's back and made a long droll face that said, "Bugs in *your* well water, too, friend." Janet grinned at her, waved to Mel, and left.

When Mary Pat had served the coffee and gone back to planting corn, Jay began, with no preliminary small talk. "You are the one man who's in a position to bring settlers to this town."

Mel raised his eyebrows but didn't answer.

"As a newspaperman, you are well aware of the power of that press." Jay made a declamatory gesture toward the scarred oak press. "With that machine you can advertise Eden City in every part of the East. Every part of the East, I say, to every man jack who ever thought about homesteading out this way. Will you use that power to its fullest?"

Mel pinched at his nose thoughtfully. "I'm not entirely sure I understand what you have in mind, Jay. Of course I want to do all I can. It's to my advantage to see this town grow."

"What I have in mind is perfectly simple. I merely want you to start getting out as many copies as you can of the—what are you calling it?"

"The Adams County Clarion."

"Don't you think The Eden City Clarion would sound more impressive? 'Adams County' has a rather countrified ring, wouldn't you say? Now, along with the paper, you must send copies of this." He withdrew a sheet of foolscap from his vest and unfolded it between them. "This is a drawing of Eden City. I worked on it all morning."

It was a large, neatly elaborate charcoal drawing with the title "Eden City, Iowa" in one corner. The view looked west along the trail toward the river, but it took Mel several minutes to orient it. In the drawing the trail was a broad, smooth, busy street. Charlie's blacksmith shop in the foreground was a brick structure, square and prosperous looking, with a sign that read "Gates Ironworks, Inc." Beyond it was a large and totally fictitious livery stable that hid all but a corner of Willard Borofen's road ranch. The bridge in the background was equally fictitious, as were the town square, courthouse, rows of stores, and streets lined with sturdy frame homes. Church steeples and a schoolhouse were conspicuously placed.

Mel blew out a long breath. "This is very impressive, but don't you think it should say 'proposed city of,' somewhere on there? I mean, this gives the impression that Wil—the town looks like this already."

Jay smiled tolerantly. "I am a city planning director, Mr. M, and believe me, this is the way it's done. If we sent pictures of it as it looks now, do you think anyone would really settle here? We attract them with this, they spend their last cent to get here, they can't afford to go back, and presto. We have a population! Once they get out here, the town'll look like this picture in no time at all, believe me."

Mel shook his head. "I don't know. It seems—not quite honest somehow. Misleading. Think how those people will feel when they get here and find . . ." He gestured toward the empty prairie.

"Mr. M, you can take my word for it, this is the way it's done. People expect a little exaggeration here and there. They take it into account. Now about the newspaper. Make these first issues impressive. Mention things like, oh, the City Council meeting last night. Dress it up, you know? Throw in a few society items. Use your imagination. Nobody in Ohio is going to know whether we really have a lyceum and debating society or not. These issues won't be circulated locally, of course. They're just for recruiting purposes, so to speak. As soon as the town treasury can afford it, you'll be reimbursed for your expenses. Do we understand each other?"

Mel frowned down at the paper he was doodling on. His pen had darkened and embellished the words "Adams County Clarion," and there were notes he had made while Janet was there. He avoided Jay's eyes.

"This isn't quite what I had in mind for my newspaper." He sighed. "Let me give it some thought."

Jay gripped his hand across the desk. "You are an intelligent and far-seeing man, Mr. M, and I have every faith that you'll do what's best in the long run for Eden City. I'm going down to the land office tomorrow to file on the quarter section just east of the township land. I'll take this drawing along and get it lithographed so you can have copies of it to send along with your first edition."

As Jay's buggy disappeared over the hill, Mel swore softly. The cabin seemed suddenly cluttered and stifling. He rose and went outside. "Ought to give poor Pat a hand with the corn, anyhow."

That night when they went to bed, he told Mary Pat

about Jay's proposal. He'd kept away from the subject while Muffin and Jason were underfoot, but he knew she'd have to hear it.

Their bedroom was a small lean-to, built on behind the cabin's main room. The walls had lost much of the mud chinking between the logs, so that on a clear night the stars showed through. The floor was only clay from the riverbank, but the room did have one window, small and high, but paned with glass. It was open tonight. A fragrant moist breeze filled the new curtains and carried the soft night sounds—cicadas and frogs and a faint cooing that might have been either birds or Indians.

He lay face down on the feather bed, arms above his head, while his wife sat beside him and kneaded the stiffness out of his shoulders. Her practiced hands lulled him. He would much rather have drifted off to sleep than continue telling her about Jay.

"Go on," Mary Pat urged. "What did he say after you told him it sounded dishonest?"

"I didn't exactly say *dishonest*. That's too strong a word. I thought it was a little misleading, when he first told me about it. But I don't know, this is his profession after all, and I assume he knows what he's doing. I was thinking afterward, though, there's no reason why I shouldn't do the promotion paper he wants for back east, and also do the regular local newspaper as I'd planned."

"Mmm. That sounds like a good solution." With a final slap, she ended the massage, and in minutes she was asleep. It took Mel much longer.

It was a glaring afternoon in early July. Another new family had arrived the day before, and Janet was cutting a diagonal path across the town square with a welcome offering from her mother—a crock of hominy, still steaming, and a pan of Vesta's special apple corn bread. She moved slowly, partly because the day was so heavily hot and partly because she still felt traces of childish reluctance at meeting new people. Her eighteenth birthday had passed the week before, and yet it seemed to her that the poise of maturity was as far away as it had always been.

In the middle of the square she turned and walked backwards, even more slowly. From this exact spot the new two-story front on Charlie's blacksmith shop looked convincing; one step in either direction revealed the fact that the building behind the new sawed-plank front was still the low shed it had always been, made of spindly, poorly chinked logs.

The town square was still little more than a level plot of waist-high prairie grass, but by now it had been surveyed by government men from the land office and had been marked off from the open prairie by rows of tall poles topped by strips of red flannel. Janet smiled as she noticed the poles along the south side. Their red flannel banners had once again disappeared in the night. "Some Indian woman's got herself some fancy hair ribbons today," she muttered. "This town's going broke buying red flannel."

Along the north side of the square ran the old trail,

which Jay insisted was now Adams Street. On the northeast corner of the square was the pride of the town, a two-story brick hotel that, when completed, would have eight rooms upstairs, each with its own window; a dining room with a glass chandelier from St. Louis; and a lobby with genuine velvet drapes.

Even though the building was not yet complete, it was already in use as a meeting place. Now, on the Sundays when the circuit rider was in town, he held church services in the hotel dining room rather than in private homes as before.

The hotel's proprietors had made this offer as soon as they arrived from Illinois. Miss Trumble and her brother wanted the hotel to be the center of things right away.

Besides Charlie's shop and the hotel, the square now had four houses and two business establishments. The houses were Jay Zupin's tin-and-tar-paper shack that just barely met the minimum homestead requirements that allowed him to claim the land along the south side of the square, plus three log-and-sod huts built on land bought from Jay. Next to the hotel was a saloon built of canvas over poles, with a crudely lettered sign that read "Hostetter's Bitters, Nature's Wonder Cure, Drink It Here or Take It Home." Next to the saloon was Janet's destination, a de-wheeled covered wagon that would evolve into a hardware, harness, and seed store.

She was almost there when she heard Mel call her

name. Her face reddened at the secret knowledge that she'd been hoping to see him this afternoon. She stopped and waited for him to ride up beside her.

"Where are you headed for?" He smiled down from the brilliant sky. The sun, just behind his head, brought tears to Janet's eyes and blurred his features when she tried to look up at him. His shirt was so white that somehow she knew he would smell good in spite of the heat and the horse, if she were close enough to smell him. Tied to his saddle was a burlap sack of rolled copies of the *Clarion*.

She looked away from the sun and said, "Over to the new people's. Ma and I lyed a batch of hominy this morning, and Ma made up some of her apple corn bread. Smell." She held up the crock and pan, and he leaned far out of his saddle to inhale their vapors.

"Umm, that's ambrosia, Miss Borofen. With a mother like that to learn from, you're going to make some young man a mighty good wife one of these days. Here, take this along to the new family, compliments of the editor." He handed down a copy of the *Clarion*.

"I will. Thanks."

"Mary Pat's on her way over to your house to help your ma with the quilt, so she's got your copies. Oh, and Janny, be sure you read this week's poem. I chose it especially with you in mind."

He had already turned and trotted away before she could think of an appropriate answer. Setting down her

dishes, she dropped cross-legged to the ground and unfolded the single-sheet newspaper. The Poet's Corner
was at the bottom of the last page. Her heart pounded in
her ears as she read:

In May, when sea-winds pierced our solitudes,
I found the fresh Rhodora in the woods,
Spreading its leafless blooms in a damp nook,
To please the desert and the sluggish brook.
The purple petals, fallen in the pool,
Made the black water with their beauty gay;
Here might the red-bird come his plumes to cool,
And court the flower that cheapens his array.
Rhodora! if the sages ask thee why
This charm is wasted on the earth and sky,
Tell them, dear, that if eyes were made for seeing,
Then Beauty is its own excuse for being:
Why thou wert there, O rival of the rose!
I never thought to ask, I never knew:
But, in my simple ignorance, suppose
The self-same Power that brought me there brought you.

Again she read it, and again and again, ignoring the
first half and concentrating on the last part, where she
felt the kernel of the thing was. At first it was just words,
rhythmic, high-sounding, meaningless, as poems had always been for her in school. But it had to have a meaning, a message for her from Mel, a message all the more

personal for being distributed throughout the county. ". . . Janny, be sure you read this week's poem. I chose it especially with you in mind."

Suddenly, when it seemed all her powers of concentration were about to melt and trickle away, the meaning burst inside her head. Rhodora was a flower, blooming where no one ever went, and the man was saying what a waste it was to have such a pretty flower go unnoticed, and then the man realized that he himself had noticed it, enjoyed it, and justified its existence with his enjoyment of it. And he was teasing the rest of the world for not seeing it.

Then what was the message for me? she wondered. That I'm the flower, and he's the only one around here who appreciates me? Could that be it? *My* charm is wasted on the earth and sky . . . the self-same Power that brought me here brought him? *Could* that be it?

The grass around her was so high that it hid from her sight all signs of other people. Through her dress the earth was nearly as warm as the air against her face. For a moment she could almost feel herself becoming a flower, not a rhodora, whatever that was, but perhaps a sunflower. Then her own foolishness jolted her, and she picked up her food and went on across the square.

She introduced herself to the new family, the Wheelocks, explained the hominy and apple corn bread, handed over the *Clarion* with poorly hidden reluctance, and started home again, floating through the grass on the heady rhythm of the poem. She didn't dare dwell on whatever personal meaning Mel could have intended for her. Instead she played with the realization, almost as exciting as hidden meanings, that she, all alone without the help of a teacher or anyone else, had read a poem and understood what it meant. For the first time she began to wonder whether Mel might have been right about her when he said she had sensitivity.

An overwhelming longing swept through her to talk to somebody, to see if anybody besides Mel could recognize this new ability, this quality in her that only she and Mel knew about. But there was no one she could think of to try herself out on, so she went home.

Her mother and Mary Pat were in the sunny middle dining room, bent over the quilting frame between the tables and the fireplace, where the light was best. The quilt was the white and blue Rose of Sharon pattern that Vesta had begun last year, intending it for Del. Now it was to be donated to the new hotel.

Mary Pat looked up and smiled at Janet. "Hello. Come and join us. We can always use another pair of hands."

Without looking up, Vesta said, "Hominy get delivered all right? You didn't spill it?"

"Of course not. Mrs. Wheelock said thank you very much, she sure appreciated it, and she'll be over in a day or so, soon as they get settled." She took her place between the women and bent out over the frame. It gave her a funny feeling to be standing here beside Mary Pat. It was a slightly uncomfortable jolt back to reality.

The door beside the loft ladder stood open, letting in flies and the hot breeze. The three of them worked in easy silence, except when the song Mary Pat was humming to herself became audible. The flies droned; the three needles made small popping sounds as they pierced the taut muslin.

Janet shifted her weight to the other hip and leaned farther over the frame to begin a new row of yarn knots. She was beginning to feel as though she'd been at it forever—stitch, clip the yarn, pull it tight, and tie the knot. Stitch, clip the yarn . . .

From outside came the shouts and pounding hooves of a horse race. A month ago, even a week ago, she'd have left the quilting frame and joined the boys at the mill. Now she felt cut off from the boys and from her old familiar self. With a small chill of desolation, she glanced at her mother and felt cut off from her, too, and even from Mary Pat. Her mother's profile was such an unmoving mass that Janet knew, beyond a doubt, it hid no secret core of sensitivity. No one could ever possibly have likened Vesta Borofen to a flower wasting its charm on earth and sky. Covertly Janet searched that rock-set face for even the smallest sign of the kind of understanding that would make it possible to talk to her. It wasn't there. All Janet could see in her mother's profile was the fact that, when she matured, she was going to look a great deal like her mother. Did that mean she would have to *be* like her all the way through? she wondered.

She put Vesta out of her mind and tried to see herself as she might look at this moment to someone else, to Mel, for instance, as she bent gracefully across the quilting frame, working the knots with deft fingers, her face somehow absorbing the reflected delicacy of the Rose of Sharon pattern. Her eyes blurred out of focus as she pictured it, her back straightened to a more graceful angle, her fingers arched.

She saw a flash of motion past the open door. It was Miss Trumble, on her way around the building to the outhouse, which was still the town's only public convenience. She was a short woman of perhaps fifty, and she exuded such force that Janet often found herself leaning back, away from the blast of the woman's personality. Miss Trumble seemed to carry most of her mass in her head and shoulders, always leaning forward when she walked. Even the pile of hair atop her head, which Will Junior claimed was a wig, tipped forward over her brow. Her intensity had irritated Janet since their first meeting.

"There goes Miss Trouble," Janet whispered.

Without looking up, Vesta said, "Janet. She never did nothing to you."

But Mary Pat's eyes twinkled. "Mel was saying the other night, it wasn't any wonder she never got married.

He said a man never knew if she was going to say howdy or slug him and throw him over her shoulder."

Janet and Mary Pat laughed across the somber Vesta, but Janet had a sudden fleeting fear that Mel might have made a similar remark about her. No, surely not, not if he thought of her like that poem.

Miss Trumble chugged past again, heading back toward the road. Her back was arched: her bosom led the way while her stubby legs followed after.

Mary Pat chuckled and whispered loudly to Janet, "She's got a hitch in her git-along."

Somehow there was never a sting to Mary Pat's jibes. Her sunny spirit neutralized the acid in her words. She and Janet stitched, clipped, knotted, in the glow of friendly spite.

As she often did when they were together, Janet studied Mel's wife while they worked. The tiny waist and miniature bust; the rounded arms with their pale freckles; the sheen that lay on the backs of her hands; the uptilted nose and curly red hair—the total effect was, to Janet, the ultimate softness, brightness, femininity.

Janet sighed and absentmindedly ran the needle under a fingernail.

"Don't bleed on the quilt," Vesta said in her monotone.

Suddenly the quilt-tying became stiffling work. She muttered an excuse and wandered the length of the dining room and down the step into the cabin. Will Junior, who was supposed to be watching the store, had disappeared.

The day before, Willard had come back from Nebraska City with two wagonloads of merchandise fresh from a St. Louis freight boat. Janet examined the new things and found nothing interesting except for a bolt of white cotton eyelet so fine it was almost lace. "What'd Pa get that for?" she mumbled to herself. "Who would ever wear that in Willard's Ford?"

She hefted the bolt and carried it to the corner where the mirror was. By shoving aside the nest of buckets and washtubs and moving a keg of vinegar, she was able to see most of herself. She didn't dare lay the bolt down on any of the grimy surfaces around her, but she managed to reel off a couple of yards and hold the bolt under her arm while she draped the eyelet over her head and shoulders. She sucked in her stomach and clutched the eyelet to her waist, half turning, watching herself from the corners of her eyes. She was regal, a snow flower whose beauty was its own excuse for being.

Miss Trumble's grating voice filled the room. "Girls your size ought not to wear eyelet, Janet. Broadcloth suits you better, dear. Or linsey. My, that's impractical goods, white eyelet. Whatever possessed your father to order that, I wonder. I need a tin of saleratus, dear."

As soon as Miss Trumble was gone, Janet went outside to stand, fists on hips, in the sun. She felt exposed, as though Miss Trumble had caught her stealing, and her embarrassment made her vengeful. When she saw Will

Junior among the knot of boys in front of the mill, she shouted at him. "Get in here and mind the store like you're supposed to."

He came sidling across, fists up, ready for battle. "You goin' to make me?" He danced around her, a rather pudgy thirteen-year-old, already nearly as tall as she was.

"Listen, little brother, I could clean you out faster than greased lightning could pass a funeral. And you know it."

He danced around a little longer before he shrugged and ambled into the cabin.

Chapter Four

Mel sat with his back to the packing-crate desk, his feet on the windowsill. It took all his will power to keep his attention on the notes in his lap, with the open window and the August afternoon just beyond his feet. This week's issue of the *Adams County Clarion*, local edition, would be the first to come out of his new office, and Mel thought he could see improvement in its quality, even now in the rough-notes stage. His notes for this issue seemed more concise, more professional, than the ones he'd written in the cabin.

The office was on the second floor of the new hotel, in the front room overlooking the town square. It was a stark room, white and pungent with new plaster. The afternoon sun glared on unvarnished raw floorboards.

On the coat-tree in the corner, built for him by

Charlie Gates in honor of the new office, hung Mel's plastering overalls. In exchange for part of the office rent, he was plastering the hotel's guest rooms. Mornings he plastered; afternoons he hunted down stories, wrote them, set type, printed and distributed the weekly *Clarion*. The back-east editions were temporarily discontinued, until spring began drawing people west again next year.

Mel dropped his feet and swung around to his desk. Murmuring to himself, he sorted through the clutter of papers between his elbows.

"Let's see now, the lead story's worth a good column and a half. Then we got the slavery editorial; the poem—better use a long one this time; society news—nothing there. Oh yes, the Crows went down to Corning yesterday. And Reverend Watson will be in town next Sunday. Then there's the two ads. Now if I can pick up a story or two down at the mill tomorrow, that should fill it up." Each week he felt a wash of relief when he was sure there would be enough material to fill the single-fold paper.

He smiled down at the layouts for the two ads, those precious squares that lifted the *Clarion* from hobby status to the level of a newspaper that paid at least a part of its cost. Of course, the hotel's ad was in exchange for office rent, along with the plastering. And the Willard's Ford General Store ad only brought in two dollars a week, and that was usually paid in goods from Willard's store, rather than in cash.

Old Willard's not advertising the store, anyway, Mel thought smiling. He's advertising the name *Willard's Ford.*

He swung the chair around lazily, leaned far back, and thought about how nice it would be to have some kind of fan up there on the ceiling. His feet were on the windowsill again, his hands clasped across his stomach. A contented smile came and lingered, as he sank back and down into the luxury of his circumstances. Editor of his own paper in an up-and-coming town where, in later years, he'd be known as one of the highly respected city fathers; a sweet wife who knew how to rub his shoulders when they ached and who kept a good house, a good garden; healthy, loving children; supper waiting for him when he got home, and only an hour or so of hoeing the corn afterwards. And there was the prospect, the definite prospect, of a time when he wouldn't have to grow his own corn at all, when the paper would make so much money that the Makiniches could buy the corn someone else had to sweat over.

He tipped forward and planted his feet on the floor. Chin in hands, he stared down at the square outside the window. It was a genuine square now, since Billy Crow had plowed a road all the way around it. Two new businesses had joined the cluster on the north—a livery stable between Charlie's blacksmith shop and the Borofen's, and a cafe-saloon across the trail from the hotel on the northeast corner.

From his window Mel looked west across the waist-high grass of the square, into the black tangle of Morton's Woods. He could see the jam of wagons around the mill, the gleam of the river beyond. He saw the front of Borofen's store, where a pair of boys wrestled in a storm of dust. Directly below his window were the foreshortened figures of Willard and Charlie Gates unloading a wagonful of round-bottomed puncheon planks that were being laid in front of the hotel for a sidewalk. Miss Trumble stood on the hotel porch, watching the men.

"They ain't chinked in very tight along here, Charlie. A body could twist his ankle on them puncheons easy as fleas." Her voice rasped Mel's nerves.

Squinting against the leveling rays of the afternoon sun, he saw Janet striding across the square toward the hotel, disdaining the plowed line of Adams Street to slice through the grass. He watched with pleasure her unswerving progress that scattered the handful of pigs and chickens in her path. Just below his window she paused. Mel leaned forward on his elbows and looked directly down on her head. Charlie had turned from his planks to throw a heavily coy punch at Janet's arm, but she dodged with irritation and, Mel thought, a trace of dignity, although there was no dignity in her threat to clean Charlie out if he didn't quit bothering her.

A smile played across Mel's face. What did I tell you? he said to himself. That kid's beginning to show some promise, and all it took was my treating her like a lady, introducing her to a little good poetry. Another year or so of my influence and she's going to be quite a woman.

In the glow of self-satisfaction he closed the office and went downstairs.

Janet turned away from Charlie and her father when she heard Mel behind her. The sight of him in his editor clothes never failed to quicken her blood. Today his shirt gleamed white in the afternoon sun, his vest flashed an iridescent blue, his watch chain twinkled. Her own grubbiness intensified beside him, and subdued her.

"Hi, Janny. Want to walk over to the mill with me, and see if there's any news? How do, Willard, Charlie."

As they crossed the square, Janet matched him stride for stride. "Somebody ought to get out and scythe off this square," she said, kicking at the grass. "Get a right smart chance of hay off it if they did."

She wanted to tuck her hand in the crook of his arm and walk slower, and maybe twirl a parasol on her shoulder, and be walking on a board sidewalk instead of wading through prairie hay. Maybe, one of these days, she mused. Maybe sometime I'll know how to take a man's arm, dainty, without knocking him off his feet doing it.

"I hear you got a new admirer," Mel said suddenly, grinning down at her.

She looked away. "Got no such thing. Who'd ever admire a horse like me?"

64

"Oh, now. I admire you, Miss Borofen, and I've been hearing rumors about that young fellow staying on at your place, even though Charlie's had his wagon fixed for nearly a week now."

Janet snorted. "Oh, him. He ain't a young fellow. He's up around thirty. Oh, I didn't mean . . ." She glanced up at Mel in confusion. He laughed, and she went on. "Anyway, Mr. Kane's just staying an extra day or so, till his oxen get rested a little. He's got him a homestead in Nebraska. Went back to Chicago to get a wife." She felt her face go red.

"Did he find one?" Mel was looking down warmly at her.

"Nope. Couldn't find one that suited him. They were all too soft and spindly, he said. Said he had to give up and start back home before cold weather or the claim jumpers got him."

Suddenly Will Junior was riding toward them at a full gallop, spewing dust against the front of the new livery stable. "Hey, Mel! You better get on home. I was just out there, and Mary Pat hasn't seen Jason since lunch. She's getting awful worried. Here, take Baldy." He leaped down and flung the reins to Mel.

In an instant Mel and the horse were churning up the new road to his cabin. Janet and Will exchanged glances; then Janet yelled. "Go get Pa and Charlie. They're over by the hotel." Already she was running along the pasture hedge toward the barn. She clapped a bridle on the first horse she could catch and flung herself over his back.

When she got to the cabin, Mary Pat was standing on the ridge of the roof, shading her eyes with her hands and pivoting slowly, scanning the prairie in every direction. She nearly lost her balance turning at Janet's approach.

"Which way did Mel go?" Janet shouted.

"Straight north!"

"I'll go west then, between here and the river. Will's coming with the men. They can take south and east."

She wheeled the horse and put him at a trot, zigzagging toward the river. "That little troublemaker, wandering off in this grass. Jason! Jason!"

The wild prairie hay was at its tallest in August. The slender gray-green blades brushed the horse's chest and swished past Janet's bare legs, scratching them to the hem of her dress, which rode indecent and unnoticed above her knees. A five-year-old boy could be utterly hidden three feet away in the lush growth. The sun was at the top of the river timber now. Only another hour or so until twilight.

"Jason! Jason!" She strained her ears to hear, through the swishing of the grass, any small voice that might be calling to her.

When they came to the timber, she slowed the horse to a walk and scanned the maze of trunks and limbs and

66

shadowy underbrush. She followed the bank of the muddy little Nodaway north and south and back north again, calling. When finally she emerged from the woods and started zigzagging a different course back toward the cabin, the sun was out of sight, leaving daylight but no shadows. The grass had a lavender-pink cast now, and the sky to the east showed the night's first stars.

What's Mel thinking now? she wondered. If he was here, what would I say to him to make him feel better?

"Ja—son."

They came to the shallow ravine of the creek, with a handful of cottonwood trees lining its rim. The horse picked his way down the bank, stepping over exposed tree roots. A half-hop carried him across the trickle of creek water, and he plunged up the other bank. They turned north, and had just crested a sudden low hill when the horse sank beneath Janet, pitching her over his head.

"Darn horse, if you've gone and broke your leg . . ." She picked herself up and, fighting for the breath knocked out of her by the fall, turned to the horse. He was already on his feet, apparently unhurt.

"Well, that was lucky," she mumbled to herself, catching up the trailing reins. Then, out of curiosity, she found the hole he'd stepped in. She reached down into it and felt only empty space. "Hmm, must be a—oh sure. I remember. That old sod house. I'd forgot all about that thing."

She led the horse down the slope that wasn't a hill

but a house. On the west side of it, facing the creek, a log wall had been built against the mound of earth, with empty black squares where the door and window had been. This was the soddy's only wall. The rest of the house was hollowed out of the hillside and so overgrown that it melted into the prairie in a perfect camouflage.

Janet stuck her head through the low doorway and called to Jason, but the place had an unquestionable feeling of emptiness. She listened and peered through the dank blackness of the soddy, then mounted and started back east again.

As she rode and called and scanned the billowing prairie, she remembered when she had been not much older than Jason and the soddy had been lived in. It was just inside the boundary of Mel's land, and had been the first home of the couple who later built the Makinich cabin. Dimly, Janet recalled riding her pony back to the soddy to visit the couple. The woman had fed her molasses candy. The soddy had seemed big then.

The darkness was almost total now. Only a band of sky behind her was still pale pink and green. As she neared the cabin, she could see Mel and Mary Pat silhouetted in the lighted doorway. They stood with their arms around each other, and Mel's head was bent in a sheltering attitude over his wife's. Janet felt a small dark pain that had nothing to do with a little lost boy.

Before she had time to dismount, whoops and pounding hooves split the stillness. From beyond the cabin came half a dozen riders with Willard in the lead, and locked around Willard's waist were the small arms of Jason Makinich.

Loud voices and boisterous relief filled the cabin. All of its lanterns were lit. The searchers had been rewarded with Mary Pat's dried apple pie and the Kentucky whiskey Mel had been hoarding. Most of them had gone home by now, but still, with all the Makiniches there, plus Janet and Will Junior, Willard, Charlie, and the lingering visitor Harold Kane, the cabin offered very little standing room. Janet perched on the corner of the children's bunk and balanced her plate of pie on her knees, her feet protecting her coffee mug on the floor.

She was aware of the sweat marks and horsehairs on her dress and legs but assumed, rightly, that no one was noticing. I don't reckon I smell any worse than the rest of them, she thought.

Jason was making the rounds, excitement and exhaustion on his small face. Enduring the squeeze of his embrace was the tan puppy Mel had brought home last week.

"I got lost in the grass, and I cried," he piped. "I got lost in the grass, Janny. See? I hurt myself." He showed her a scraped knee, forgetting for the moment that it was an old wound. She admired his scab.

As she licked the last of the pie from her fingers, she

realized that Mr. Kane was staring at her from across the room. It irritated her. He'd been at it for days now, following her with open stares as she served his meals, tagging along while she did her chores, saying little but weighing her every move. His manner was the same as Pa's horse-trading customers' when they were considering a deal.

It wouldn't be so bad, she thought, if he weren't so —so red-necked and flat-faced. Or if he didn't always have a crust of manure on his boot, or if she could for one moment imagine him appreciating in her the qualities Mel saw and appreciated.

Her eyes found Mel and Mary Pat, standing by the stove. His hand was on the nape of her neck, rubbing in a rough, practiced way, and her head arched back into his hand. Both of them were watching Jason as he climbed on and off of laps around the room.

A sudden bleakness descended on Janet. If I could only find me a man like that one, she thought. A heavy sigh escaped her as she looked from Mel to Harold Kane. But am I going to have to settle for that? Or do I even deserve any better than him? Maybe I should be grateful for the chance. She shuddered. At least I'd have me a home of my own and somebody that belonged to me. Oh, this is all stupid anyway. Harold hasn't asked me, and besides, if I ever did find another one as good as Mel, I wouldn't be good enough for him.

"I got to get back and let Ma know what happened,"

she said to Mary Pat. "Thanks for the pie, and I'm just as glad as I can be that Jason's all right."

Eyes brimming, Mary Pat gave Janet's arm a squeeze. "We sure do thank you for helping, Janny." She lowered her voice to a whisper. "Come out tomorrow and I'll tell you a secret that nobody else knows except me and Mel."

As she rode away from the cabin, Janet heard another horse behind her. "Here it comes now." With dread and a little anticipation, she braced herself for his proposal.

"Janet. Wait for me. I'll see you home." Mr. Kane's horse caught up with hers, and they rode on in silence.

The new road was just a plowed strip, one wagon wide, from Mel's cabin south across the empty prairie, then between Charlie's corn patch and the Borofen's pasture hedge, to the northwest corner of the town square. The footpath that cut diagonally over to Willard's Ford was the shorter way home, but now that there was a road, Janet felt obliged to use it, especially since Mel had plowed it.

A full moon and a sky full of stars lit the way. They illuminated the man beside her, with his thick neck and mixing-bowl haircut. He rode loosely, elbows flapping, feet bobbing from his ankles.

"Janet, how'd you like to come out home with me?"

In spite of her bracing, it came as a small shock.

"I got a good place out there, got a three-room soddy

and a well right up close to the house. Not any trees around to get in the way of the wheat, just miles and miles of good flat land."

He paused, but she didn't answer.

"I looked all over Chicago, and I never saw one woman that I'd care to have out there with me. But when I saw you, you just struck me right. You remember what you was doing the first time I saw you? You was out back, wringing chicken necks and just a-whistlin' away to beat the devil. I said to myself, now there's a woman that'd be some help to her man. I been watching you all this time, and I've made up my mind to it."

Any temptation she might have felt to accept him, settle her future once and for all, get herself a home of her own and prove to Mel Makinich that someone wanted her, drained away and left her cold and empty. Harold Kane wanted her because she wasn't too fine-haired to wring chicken necks; Mel saw something much more valuable in her, or at least he said he did. Maybe Mel was wrong, or lying, but maybe he wasn't. Maybe the next man to come along would be like Mel, and if so, then there was a possibility that Janet Borofen might end up somebody entirely different from Vesta Borofen. There *was* that chance, as long as she held herself away from all the Harold Kanes.

She tried to think of something to say to him, to show him how far above him she was.

He grabbed for her hand and said, "How soon can

you leave? I already wasted five days here, and it's going to be coming on September pretty quick."

She pulled her hand away. "I ain't going to marry you."

His jaw dropped. "Well, why *not?*"

In a sudden aching fury she turned on him. "Because I got sensitivity, damn it!" She whipped her horse into a gallop and left him gaping after her.

Chapter Five

By midmorning of the next day Janet was finished with the hay beds in the loft. The job took only about half as long as it used to, now that the Adams House Hotel was in business. She descended the ladder and, hanging her pitchfork on its peg, went through the cabin and into the morning sun. In the dust of the front yard Will Junior and Billy Crow were playing catch with the four-old-cat ball and arguing the relative merits of horses and oxen.

"Yeah, but with a horse," Billy said, "you can work him all day and ride him into town at night. You can't ride a stupid old ox, or race him either."

"Yeah, but when an ox gets old, you can butcher him and have steaks. An old horse ain't nothing but an old horse."

"Yeah, but . . ."

74

Janet turned to go. She'd heard them argue this question endlessly, and on the reverse sides as often as not. As she started up the trail toward Mel's road, a wagon appeared, coming—as all wagons did—from the east. Automatically she looked to see whether it was a single man or a family. It was a family. Mildly curious, she turned and went back when the wagon passed her and stopped at the store.

She heard the man call to Will Junior and Billy. "Say there, boys, I'm a little confused. The sign at the edge of town said, 'Now entering Eden City,' but your sign, over the door there, says 'Willard's Ford, Iowa.' What the heck town is this, anyway?"

"Willard's Ford!" "Eden City!" The boys shouted in unison. By the time Janet got to them, Will and Billy had squared off and begun swinging at each other. Suddenly a shout went up from the group across the road at the mill. "A fight, everybody. Come on."

The men, bored with waiting for their turn at the mill, came streaming out of Morton's Woods. Bob Crow jumped in to help his little brother, and at the same time another boy came out of the store and leaped onto Billy's back, wrapping a thin hard arm around Billy's throat.

"Willard's Ford, Willard's Ford," Will Junior yelled.

"Eden City!"

The free-for-all was on. Janet edged around the knot of fighters, eager for a better look. Will Junior's face appeared momentarily. He crowed, "Willard's Ford," then disappeared in the dust and tumult. For a minute Janet wanted to throw herself into the abandonment of it, but glancing toward the hotel and Mel's window, she backed away. She eased around to the front wheel of the wagon and stepped up onto the hub. The view was better from there, and the dust was thinner.

The fighters were now loosely paired off into six or seven pairs, as nearly as Janet could count. Occasionally someone shouted one of the town's names, but for the most part they fought without the burden of a cause.

"We sure didn't mean to start trouble," the wagon driver shouted into Janet's ear. "All I wanted to know was what town this was. I have this lithograph picture of Eden City, so I know this couldn't be . . ."

Suddenly Jay Zupin materialized out of the dust that enveloped the wagon. "Welcome to our fair city." His voice retained its musical quality even above the shouts and grunts and thuds. "It really doesn't matter what name the city is known by, does it, my friend? Not when it's a city of such natural advantages as ours. I see you have your worldly belongings in your wagon. Probably you've heard exaggerated claims about the advantages of the Nebraska Territory. Am I right? My friends, let me tell you . . ."

Janet stepped down. She left Jay to make his pitch and her brother to do battle for the family name, and headed for the Makinich cabin. It was a hot walk. The clods of the plowed road broke under her feet, and grasshoppers rose before her with every step. The sky was cloudless and intensely blue.

She found Mary Pat in the garden with Muffin, digging potatoes. Jason ran toward her, his puppy at his heels. "I can't go any farther than that tree and that tree, or Ma'll spank me good," he announced.

Mary Pat rose when she saw Janet, and motioned her into the cabin, calling back over her shoulder, "Get three or four more big ones, Muffy; then you can stop. Come on in, Janet. Let's sit down for a minute. I'm worn out."

Quizzically Janet studied her. The usually sunny face looked almost haggard this morning. Her voice was flat; the brightness in her eyes had a strained quality. For an instant as they sat down, Janet thought Mary Pat was going to reach for her hand.

She spoke quickly. "What was the secret you were going to tell me?"

Mary Pat ran her tongue across her lips and focused her eyes somewhere beyond Janet. Brightly she said, "I'm going to have a baby, that's what. I've only been sure a couple of days now, and Mel and I both wanted you to be the first person we told. Isn't it wonderful?"

Janet was confused. From the way Mary Pat looked, she'd expected some kind of bad news. A baby was definitely not bad news, nor even much of a surprise. "I'm real happy for you," she exclaimed. "I bet Mel was just as pleased as could be, wasn't he? When is it coming?"

"About March. Yes, Mel was like a little boy himself when I told him. He was so gentle with me." Suddenly her voice broke and became a whispered rush. "Janny, I'm so scared. I was scared with Muffy, and twice as scared with Jase, and this is even worse. I've been so sick, and I get nervous whenever Mel leaves."

It was Janet who, unconsciously, took Mary Pat's hand and squeezed it hard. "Now you're being silly, Mary Pat. I remember when Ma had Will Junior, and it wasn't anything. She says it's just a hard bellyache and then a good feeling when it's over. Think about the two you got. They were worth the bellyaches, weren't they?" Disconcerted at Mary Pat's tear-filled eyes, she let go of her hand, thinking she'd squeezed too hard and hurt it.

Mary Pat smiled a sheepish damp smile and sniffed. "Listen, Janet, I know I'm being a baby about this. I can't help it. It's just that—well, just between you and me, and please don't tell Mel—I get this idea in my head every time I get pregnant, that I'm—not going to live through it. And with the baby coming in March, we might be snowed in so bad the doctor can't get out here. Would you mind coming out and staying here for a week or so when the time comes? It'd be such a relief if you could take care of the kids till I get my strength back. And if you were here when—it happened—I'd be so glad. You're a good person to hang onto. Mel's worthless when the pain comes."

78

A wave of tenderness went through Janet and left her feeling mature, capable. "You couldn't keep me away with a stick. And if we can't get you a doctor, you still got nothing to worry about. Ma's delivered a couple of dozen babies, and she's never lost a one."

Before Janet left, the two of them were laughing, and the fear, at least for the time being, was gone from Mary Pat's eyes.

A few days later, with an empty afternoon ahead, Janet took the petticoat kindling sack and started north through the river timber to see if the hazelnuts were ripe yet. She followed the Indian path along the bank. The Nodaway River was no wider than eight or ten feet here, but even in August the bed was deep and the flow powerful enough to keep the mill wheel turning. The mud banks were undercut and fringed with exposed tree roots. Sheltering the path were ancient cottonwoods and oaks, tall enough and dense enough to shade to death most of the undergrowth and leave a forest floor of moss and matted leaves.

It had been an ideal place for a child to play, Janet recalled. Among the trees she could lose sight of home completely and get herself deliciously lost, and still know that by following the river downstream she couldn't fail to find the trail and home. The timber was perpetually dark and cool, with Indians imagined or sometimes real moving from tree to tree just ahead or behind her.

As her feet followed the path automatically, she pretended Mel was walking with her. No, not Mel—she corrected the image—but the nameless ethereal man who would be everything Mel was, and would belong to her. In the privacy of the timber, out of sight of her family and Miss Trumble, Janet slowed her stride, carried herself more proudly. She wadded the kindling sack under one arm and lifted the other hand to lay it on her man's sleeve.

"Janet, you are a lovely woman." The imagined voice was so real that for a moment her heart thudded. In the shadowy stillness her face reddened. She dropped her hand and walked faster.

The hazel tree grew at the fork where a small creek joined the river, the same creek she had crossed a few nights ago, looking for Jason. It reminded her of the sod house. Since the nuts were obviously not ready to gather yet, she decided to go have another look at the soddy. She followed the creek and was out in the sun a few minutes later.

This quarter section, just north of Willard's and just west of Mel's, was still unclaimed. When Will Junior was born, Willard made a rather expensive agreement with the land-office agent that this section would be held until Will Junior was of age to claim it. It would be an excellent piece of land, half timber and half open flat cropland, close enough to the growing city of Willard's Ford, or Eden City, to be potentially valuable.

The creek led her indirectly northeast. At the spot

where the unclaimed land met Mel's, she saw the soddy. It was well camouflaged, even in the daylight, by cottonwood trees growing tall and thick around it.

Before she went inside, Janet circled the grassy mound and climbed it. It was a little taller than she was at its highest point and was ten or twelve feet across, a roughly circular mound except for the flat log-walled side. Two holes showed through the long grass on the top of the mound. One was the place where her horse had broken through; the other, lined with tin, was the remains of a stovepipe chimney.

"Lucky that old horse didn't step in the chimney," she said aloud. "He'd have broke a leg in there, for sure. Lucky I didn't step in it, for that matter."

She descended the hill and went around to the front. A tiny sheltered clearing separated the house from the creek bank a few yards away. Huge cottonwoods framed the clearing, squaring it off and protecting it. In the mud of the creek bank Janet found a barrel sunk to its rim to form a shallow well. It was half full, even now in mid-August.

She dropped to her knees and reached down to rake from the water's surface a scum of soggy leaves and cottonwood fluff. When the water was cleared and still, she could make out her face in its murky mirror. Fascinated, she leaned closer to study herself. Somehow this image was more flattering than the one the warped mirror in the store showed her, perhaps because the water softened the lines. Or was it beginning to show up? she wondered. Maybe whatever Mel saw in her really did exist and other people would begin seeing it, too. She leaned over the barrel well until the blood rushing to her head made her dizzy.

Finally she got up and turned her attention to the soddy. The door of hand-hewn planks hung from its one remaining leather hinge, and whatever had been used to cover the window was gone. Stooping, Janet went through the narrow doorway. It was several seconds before her eyes adjusted to the blackness of the room. When they did, she saw a packing-crate table in the center of the tiny cave, the bare slats of a corner bunk, a stovepipe that dangled, stoveless, from the ceiling. The rat-gnawed remains of a buffalo hide hung on one wall, covering cupboards, she guessed. Wisps of hay showed here and there on the earth floor.

As she moved into the room, she was forced to stoop and hold her head to one side to avoid the hanging tendrils of grass roots that brushed her hair. From behind her came the soft rain of dirt her head dislodged from the roots. Beside the table she found a chair hollowed from a stump. She rolled it out and sat down, facing the doorway.

For a long time she sat that way, looking at the trees through the frame of the door. Slowly she began to imagine the room scrubbed clean, with red curtains on the window and fresh hay on the floor. A stove behind her, with supper fixing. A bigger window maybe, a door with good hinges. Plenty of lamps.

Across the table sat her man, smiling, being gentle with her because of the baby coming. He'd be a big man, she thought. Fine-haired. He'd use the right words when he talked, and he wouldn't be ashamed to talk about poetry and things like that. He wouldn't be embarrassed, being gentle with her either. And he'd have another job, in town, and not just be a farmer. His name might be something like—James.

The vision of him came with startling clarity, for even though her childhood was an unusually lonely one, Janet had never had the sort of imagination that gave birth to pretend playmates. He sat there with her in the soddy, splendid in his white ruffled shirt and paisley vest, radiating intelligence and love.

In the shelter of the soddy, in the warmth of approval that came from the imagined James, the softness that started with Mel's words stirred again inside her. Just then she looked a little less like her mother.

Walking home later, kicking through the grass, Janet thought about the first tiny pastel flowers that try to survive through the spring and into the summer. If they escape all the hooves and wheels and careless feet that come their way, eventually they become strong enough and large enough to withstand the traffic. Some of the dreaminess of the soddy was still with her, and suddenly she saw her new softer self as one of these fragile spring flowers. If only she could keep herself away from the careless feet until she was strong enough to survive them!

During the weeks that followed, Janet spent as many afternoons as possible at the sod house. The sumac clumps along the river turned brick red, the cottonwoods' leaves faded, the creek and the barrel well filled with September rains. Autumn flowers covered the hump of the soddy with purple and gold.

Without asking herself why she was doing it, Janet swept out the soddy with a broom she made of shredded willow whips. She knocked down the worst of the loose dirt from the rooty ceiling and swept it outside, breaking off as many roots as she could. She got a strip of leather and some nails from Charlie and fixed the door hinge. She rearranged the table and chair, setting them beside the log wall under the window. A handful at a time, she tore up long swatches of prairie hay, flowers and all, to cover the floor. When it rained and the mud streamed down from the ceiling and poured off the roots onto everything, she cleaned the soddy out again and pulled fresh hay.

One day she realized the job of pulling hay didn't hurt her hands, didn't penetrate their toughened skin. The next morning she got a pair of work gloves from the store and smuggled them out to the soddy under the front of her dress. After that, the gloves stayed on the shelf in the soddy, behind the buffalo robe. She wore them for any job that might add to her callouses.

Janet stood patiently while Mary Pat basted her side seam. One arm was raised, out of Mary Pat's way; with the other hand she held the buttonless bodice in place. She looked down at herself. Instead of the familiar gray-brown homespun stretching away to the floor, there was a magnificent cascade of soft butter-yellow watered silk.

"Arm up," Mary Pat commanded.

Her arm was aching heavily, but she raised it again to shoulder level.

"Ouch!" Mary Pat's needle pricked her side.

"Sorry."

"I hope you're not sewing that to my shift."

Mary Pat chuckled. "I hope so, too."

The feel of the silk against her skin had an intoxi-cating effect on Janet. She felt as though the very pores of her skin were refined, her eyes enlarged and darkened, her mouth softened.

If I can't look pretty in this dress, she thought, then there's no hope for me. I'll probably never look this good again as long as I live.

"There, that should do it," Mary Pat said. "Bring me the scissors, Muff."

Cautiously, reluctantly, Janet slipped out of the dress and back into her homespun. The two women lined their chairs up along the path of sunlight that poured in through the open door, and sat down with needles and thread and laps full of silk. Muffin took her place on the floor in front of them, sitting cross-legged and waving her willow whip flyswatter around the women's faces. On the sun-warmed floorboards near Muffin's knee, the puppy sighed and twitched and slept.

Mary Pat's dress was watered silk too, a bright apple-green that complimented her auburn curls. It would be empire style, to hide the growing thickness of her waist. She had begun planning both of their dresses the minute Janet told her Miss Trumble was going to have a dance party some time next month, as soon as the hotel's chandelier arrived from St. Louis. Janet had been relieved at Mary Pat's offer to help choose the material for her dress and to lend a hand with the designing and fitting. As it worked out, the only part of the job that Janet had had the courage to try was the seam-sewing, but Mary Pat hadn't minded. It was a pleasant way to get her mind off the coming baby, and she'd enjoyed the challenge of picking out the kind of neckline and sleeves that would be most flattering to Janet.

The seam-sewing was tedious, but Janet enjoyed it. As long as she followed Mary Pat's basting stitches, there was no possible way she could go wrong. Her stitches tended to get a little out of line every now and then, but by squinting and bending low over her lap, she managed to keep them going fairly straight. Occasionally she bent too low and got in the way of Muffin's flyswatting.

She just had time to finish one side seam when Mary Pat stretched and flexed her fingers and announced that it was time to get Mel's supper started. Carefully Janet folded the dress into Mary Pat's sewing chest and started toward home.

There was enough October chill in the air to make her wish she'd worn her afghan, or at least her shoes. The sky was a bank of soft clouds, so blue they might almost be mistaken for sky at first glance. Over the muted fawn colors of the prairie hay and Charlie's cornfield lay the glow of a sun not completely cloud-hidden. The quiet radiance of the fields gave depth and brilliance to the blue clouds, separated from them only by the narrow brown stripe of the river timber. The nearly unnoticed loveliness of her prairie brought her slowly to a stop. She ached for—something.

The moment passed and she went on, but now she moved more fluidly over the rough road. Suddenly a darting prairie hen caught her eye, and she saw, between the road and Charlie's cornfield, a scattering of unfamiliar plants.

Wonder what those are, she thought. Funny I never noticed them before.

She knelt, still under the spell of the twilight and the silk dress, to study one of the plants. It was about knee high, a dead dry stalk with furled leaves as dry and colorless as their stalk. It would have been a thoroughly homely plant except for the pods. There were three of them, about three inches long and as covered with spines as a horned toad. They were a pale silvery gray-brown, the same color as her dress. The bottom pod was sealed tight, the middle one open a crack, but it was the highest pod that held Janet's gaze. It had burst wide, and from the coarse drab shell rose a cloud of spun-silver gossamer. Looking closer, she saw tiny russet seeds attached here and there to the fluff, waiting for their final release, a flight on a guest of wind to the waiting earth.

Breathless at the unexpected delicacy, Janet sat down on the grass and reached to touch the fluff. She was aware that Mel was coming toward her, headed home for supper, but she remained as she was. He left the road and stood over her.

"Look at this, Mel. Isn't that the softest stuff you ever felt? What are these, anyway?"

He knelt down beside her. "Milkweeds. We had some around Muscatine when I lived there." His voice softened as he picked up her mood. "They come west with the seed corn, I expect. Probably in a few years they'll be all over this part of the state, them and other weeds. I always kind of liked the milkweeds though, hard and ugly on the outside and yet so soft inside." His voice trailed into silence as he reached past her to cup the pod in his hand and stroke the silver fluff with the ball of his thumb.

Looking at him, Janet felt her eyes go soft. The moment was suspended, as suffused with light as the golden fields around them. She heard herself say, "Maybe they *have* to be tough and ugly on the outside, so that soft inside part won't get hurt."

He didn't answer, but the look he gave her was a welcome to his level, an acknowledgement that she, too, had theories about things. She felt beautiful.

She looked down in sudden embarrassment, and at that instant his hand tightened around the pod, and his thumb gouged it and flipped the downy floss into the breeze.

"No!" She grabbed his wrist, but the harm was done. She looked away from the barren pod and felt for a moment as though his thoughtless destruction had emptied her, too.

"Hey, Janny." His voice was softly quizzical. His finger lifted her chin. "There's plenty more milkweeds. Look over there by the corn. And this time next year you'll have milkweeds all over the place."

Embarrassed, she smiled away from his face. When he offered his hand to help her up, she took it and rose, swatting roughly at the grass on the seat of her dress. They talked for a few minutes about the progress of the silk dresses; then, awkward again, they said so long and walked away from each other.

But it wasn't until much later that Janet was able to lose the small sour feeling that he had let her down.

Chapter Six

The November town meeting was the last to be held in the Borofens' dining room. Despite Willard's objections, Jay announced that because of the growing population future meetings would be held at the hotel. He went on to say that the Trumbles had received word that the glass chandelier for the dining room had left St. Louis and should arrive within two weeks, so the dance party would be held on schedule, November twentieth.

Janet's attention wandered from Jay to the dance party, to the yellow silk dress and the transformed Janet Borofen who, with the help of the dress, would become as visible to Pa and the whole town as she now was to herself, and occasionally to Mel. A yellow butterfly hidden for eighteen years in her cocoon; gossamer fluff blowing out of a milkweed pod. She wished Mel could know how poetic her thoughts were sometimes.

But of course the dance party wouldn't turn out that way. Things never did. One cautious step out of character—character born of self-defense years ago and fostered by Pa, by everyone who knew her—and someone was sure to come along and mock her and say "A girl like you ought not to wear yellow silk, dear; gunnysacks suit you better."

She tossed her head to get rid of her plaguing thoughts, and looked around the room. With each town meeting since the first one last April, the crowd in the dining room had increased until tonight the room was as full as it could possibly be. All the children sat on the floor, while the women squeezed together on the four backless benches. The men, with Janet among them, stood around and behind the benches, shoulder to shoulder and belly to backbone.

To fight the piercing chill of the November night, Willard had built a good-sized fire behind the wagon-box speaker's stand. Consequently Jay conducted the meeting in his shirt sleeves and spent a good deal of his time patting the sweat from his face. Those in the back of the room breathed warm, incredibly stuffy air, while cold drafts from beneath the poorly fitted doors blew around their ankles.

In his role as the town company's treasurer, Willard stood to give his financial report. "We're in good shape," he said. "Shares of the town company's stock have been selling pretty well back east, thanks to the fine work Mel's been doing with the *Clarion*. No income this month from the sale of business property or home lots, but that's to be expected, this time of the year."

He recited the month's expenses: fifty cents for paint to fix the town signs out along the trail—he glossed over this item, though everyone knew it was his son who had changed the "now" to "not," so the signs read "You are not entering Eden City, Iowa"; one hundred eighteen dollars to Mel Makinich for printing expenses for the back-east *Clarion;* eighty-four dollars in commissions for the agent Jay had hired to meet west-bound river travelers at Nebraska City and persuade them to settle in Eden City. Willard totaled the expenses and income, and turned the meeting back to Jay.

"Any old business?" Jay scanned the room.

"Yeah," someone bellowed. "We got to put a stop to that business of horse racing down Adams Street. It's a danged dangerous nuisance."

"That's *new* business," Jay said with resignation. "Oh well. Any suggestions, anyone?"

"Make a law agin it."

"How about diggin' a deep trench clear across the road. That'd stop 'em."

"Let's build us a jailhouse."

Suggestions were offered with increasing hilarity and decreasing helpfulness, until Jay shouted for silence.

"All right. I'm president of this town company, and I say, Billy Crow and Will Borofen Junior and any of the rest of you, stop racing your horses in the public road before you kill somebody! You got a whole empty prairie out there to tear around on. Any other new business?"

He paused, then went on. "I've talked this over with Willard and Mel and Alf Trumble, and we've decided the time has come to petition to the government for a post office here in Eden City. Now, the only thing holding us up is this childish bickering about the name." A low murmur of dissent rose. "A few of our good people here still insist on hanging onto the old name of Willard's Ford. Gentlemen, for the good of the whole community, I ask you to give up on it, so we can proceed with getting a post office."

Before Jay's mouth was closed, Willard was on the speaker's stand, protesting angrily. Throughout the room close-packed men and women took up the argument, turning toward each other, gesturing where there was room enough to, and raising their voices. From the pile of children on the floor near Jay, a frightened wail rose, and then another. Through the din someone began to shout, "Take a vote, take a vote."

"All right," Jay yelled. "We'll take a vote."

The bedlam receded. Mothers reassured their frightened children while Jay and Willard, Janet and Will Junior, worked their way through the mob, passing out paper from the supply in the store. When Willard's boot was passed and filled with ballots, then emptied and the votes counted by Vesta—with Jay watching over her shoulder—the total, from the hundred and twelve voters in the room, was Eden City, ninety-eight; Willard's Ford, one hundred and two.

"Crooked vote!" the cries rang out. "Boot stuffers!"

When Jay was finally able to make himself heard, he said, "Next meeting we'll take another vote, and with only *one* vote to a person! Meeting adjourned."

During the socializing that followed, the name battle was set aside, fortunately. The room was too crowded to have allowed for much ill feeling.

Janet moved with the tide of elbows and shoulders until she was beside Mel and Mary Pat. A homesteader from downriver edged past her and said, "You be sure and save me a dance at the stomperoo, Miz Borofen."

She flushed and nodded at him, but he was already out of sight in the shifting mass of bodies. Mel's eyes met hers. He smiled.

"Are you going to save me a dance, Janny?"

Mary Pat smiled from Mel to Janet, humoring him, secure in her place under his arm.

Suddenly Willard was behind Mel, whacking his shoulder. The joviality of hosting had reddened his face and strengthened his voice. "You *volunteering* to dance with my Janet?" he roared. "Hah!" Another shoulder whack punctuated his words. He disappeared into the crowd.

Janet stared after him with pure hate in her eyes. The fact that she knew she was a clumsy dancer added barbs to his playful thrust. Evading Mel's eyes, she turned and wove across the room, turning sideways again and again to get around people. With difficulty she got through the door that led to the bedrooms.

Why don't they all shut up and go home, she thought, aiming her irrational anger at the whole town. She felt utterly weary. She flung her dress across the blackness of the room and pulled her flannel nightgown down over her winter shift. Her hand automatically found her long wool bed stockings and drew them on. She crawled under the quilts and worked her shoulders deep into the hay mattress, squirming until her body was entrenched in a valley of hay. The quilts covered part of her face, so the cold wind, searching through the warped wall boards, found only her nose and brow to chill.

Now that she was settled, she began to strain her ears toward the voices out there. She resented that they were all having a good time while she lay, alone and probably not even missed, in her room. The longer she lay there, the more irritating the voices became, in contrast to the stillness of her room.

She thought of Mel's words: "Are you going to save me a dance, Janny?" Why did he have to say it when Mary Pat was there? Didn't it mean any more to him than that? For the first time Janet felt a small sore resentment toward Mary Pat—smiling, secure Mary Pat who never did anything clumsily, who never seriously thought a mean thought about anyone. A man couldn't help loving somebody like Mary Pat.

A sharp hay stem worked its way through the canvas mattress cover, through her nightgown and shift, to dig at the tender skin between her shoulder blades. She tossed onto her side.

"You *volunteering* to dance with my Janet? Hah!"

She tossed again and threw a sudden furious punch into the mattress. After a while she sat up and, leaning over the foot of the bed, opened the trunk. In the darkness her fingers found the little braided-hair ring in the back bottom corner of the trunk, and brought it out. The cracks in the wall let in only enough starlight to glow dimly along the silver curve of the ring.

Holding the tiny, delicate thing, she felt a sudden poignant longing. A trembling finger traced the silver circle.

I'm not what you think I am, she cried to a disbelieving, uninterested world. I'm not really like I am on the outside. Mel's the only one who knows! She felt an overwhelming need to get to the safety of the soddy, but there was no way out of the house except through the crowd. She lay back down again and squeezed the ring in her calloused fist.

"What's ailing Janet any more? Seems like she's getting touchy as a danged civet cat." Willard sat on the bed to pull off his boots. The little Betty lamp on the bureau threw long wavering shadows across the room, harshly outlining the bedstead, the planks of the walls, the row of clothes pegs, and Vesta, who sat at the lowboy pulling pins out of her hair.

When she replied with a silent shrug, he went on. "All I did was tease her a little about her dancing, and she gave me a look that'd preserve meat all summer. That kid don't have near the sense of humor she used to. What do you suppose is ailing her?"

Vesta began plaiting her hair into its nighttime braid. "Nothing's the matter with Janet. She's just like I was at her age."

"You suppose she's beginning to worry about being an old maid? Might be a good idea if she did start to do a little worrying along those lines. She ain't getting any younger."

Vesta yawned. "Oh, she's still gettin' a proposal ever' now and again. She'll give up being so picky after while and settle down with one of them. We got nothing to worry about as long as the woman shortage lasts hereabouts. Remember, Del didn't have no trouble making a good match. Course, that's the advantage of living right on the trail like we do. Plenty of men passing through. Del got her a doctor that way, and Janet'll likely get some kind of a husband."

She rolled into bed beside Willard and closed her eyes so he'd quit bothering her with his talk. Janet's moods! All that girl needed was more work to keep her occupied. The thought of Janet having moods was unsettling to Vesta. It suggested problems that might demand a mother's wisdom. The possibility frightened her in the same way that customers in the store frightened her, when the kids weren't there to wait on them. The incomprehensible jumble of merchandise, the intricacies of prices and change-making, overwhelmed her and froze her mind into mute stupidity. And problems with Janet were even worse. Thank goodness Del got married early and the boy was Willard's lookout. With any luck, maybe Janet would get married pretty soon, and then she could relax. Vesta's face loosened a little as her mind drifted back into pleasanter channels. That good ham shank for dinner tomorrow . . .

Willard turned his head to study his wife's profile. The hard planes of it, the look of quiet strength, reassured him. If Janet was having problems, her mother would take care of them.

As he sank toward sleep, his mind wandered back over the meeting. If we're going to have an honest vote on the names next meeting, he thought, I better buckle down and do some campaigning. He smiled suddenly. That darn kid, painting out the Eden City signs. That's a smart son I got myself all right. He chuckled aloud, but Vesta was already asleep and didn't hear him.

The glass chandelier arrived only a few weeks late, on the last boat up from St. Louis before the river froze for the winter. With the chandelier installed and the last of the rooms plastered, the Adams House Hotel was ready for its grand opening dance party. The *Clarion* carried the announcement as its feature story.

For two days before the big night, every woman in town was at the hotel, scrubbing, making up the beds in the hotel's bedrooms for any of the partygoers who wanted to stay over, weaving and hanging evergreen garlands, cleaning chickens. Mary Pat was by now visibly swollen with the coming baby, so she was given the sitting-down job of weaving the evergreen garlands.

Janet spent a full afternoon working her way around the walls of the combination ballroom-dining room, using a battered tin spoon to scrape the wainscoting boards clean of the hardened plaster drippings Mel had left when he plastered the room a few days before. She enjoyed the job. It was pleasantly tedious, the results were visible and satisfying, and it gave her a feeling of partnership with Mel.

Although it was unseasonably warm outside, the women kept a high fire in the fireplace in an attempt to hurry the final drying of the plaster. Janet worked at a leisurely pace, lulled by the monotony of the job and the heavy warmth of the air. She made no attempt to join the conversations behind her, but enjoyed the sound of them, Mary Pat and Mrs. Crow and the others.

I am a woman, she thought. I'm one of them. This is my place, not outside with the men. And tonight . . .

But when night came, she felt oddly depressed, almost reluctant to go. She walked across the square alone, a few minutes after the rest of the family. They had thought she was silly when she made excuses for lingering, but it was important to her that her parents not be right there at her elbow when she came in.

All afternoon the air had grown steadily colder until now Janet's breath puffed white against the black night. She clutched the afghan shawl under her chin. Her hair, freed from its knot and held only by a band of leftover yellow silk, blew across her face. On her finger was the braid-ring. Although the ground was frozen, she held her skirt high as she walked, exposing the brown bulk of her cowhide shoes. Seeing the shoes flash beneath her, Janet wished for a moment that they were more in keeping with the silk dress. "Oh well," she said with a sigh, "any shoes'd look like cowhide on those feet."

She made her way around the buggies and wagons that clogged the corner of the square, and went inside. At the doorway to the ballroom she stopped, forgetting herself for an instant at the sight—men in boiled calico shirts, their faces nicked and scraped but beaming; women, radiant in dresses made special for tonight, dresses made of treasured draperies from the old home back east, dresses made from scraps and hand-me-downs or from bolts of new goods from Willard's store. Each dress was such a glorious change from its wearer's everyday garment that it lit the face above it and came as near to lend-ing beauty as a dress can. Children were everywhere, greased down and charged up, darting between and beneath their elders, their kitchen haircuts laid low with ham fat gravy.

High above, from the middle of the vaulted ceiling, two hundred candles in the glass chandelier threw a dancing rainbow of light on the center of the room, while the edges were lit only by inadequate coal-oil lamps hung along the walls. Mary Pat's evergreen garlands encircled the room, pointed up by mammoth bows of red flannel donated by the town company from the supply used for lot-marker strips. The air that greeted Janet was spiced with pungent evergreen, damp plaster, and ham fat gravy.

She edged her way along the wall to a spot where she was more or less out of the dancers' way. I bet the wind messed up my hair, she fretted, raking her hands through the loose strands. The ring was an unaccustomed bulk between her fingers, and the silk of her dress no longer felt intoxicating against her skin. Now it seemed alien, brittle, so fragile it might rip if she made a sudden move. She was uncomfortably aware of the expanse of bare skin showing above the dress, although Mary Pat had assured her the neckline was completely proper.

She watched the dancers. There was Mel, beautiful in his white shirt and paisley vest, dancing with his small daughter, who glowed and puffed in an effort to keep up with him. There was Miss Trumble whirling with the owner of one of the saloons. Janet stared at her in sur-

101

prise. Miss Trumble's dress was made of the lacelike white eyelet. So that's who bought that bolt, Janet thought wryly.

Willard danced past in the loose embrace of Charlie Gates. Charlie wore a red bandana on his arm, signifying that he was the girl, according to the custom here, where women were so scarce. Both men roared with laughter, pumped their elbows, and flung their legs in a boisterous caricature of a dance.

Pa's been to the bar already, looks like, Janet thought. She looked for her mother and saw her seated in a far dark corner, being talked at by a woman Janet didn't recognize. Mary Pat was sitting down, too, but her chair was on the bright edge of the dance floor. Her face was radiant above the bulk of her lap.

Ma wasn't having a good time. Janet could feel it, clear across the dance floor. Vesta's face was always as expressionless as it was now, but there was a defensiveness in the set of her shoulders that told Janet her mother was wishing herself back in her own kitchen. Janet's shoulders set themselves that way too, sometimes, curving up and forward. She found they were doing it now and, frowning, forced them down where they belonged.

As she looked from her mother to Mary Pat, who was laughing up into the face of a young man standing beside her chair, Janet wondered almost desperately whether it really was possible to change the kind of person you were, just by deciding to be another kind. She was committed, with all her strength, to making herself like Mary Pat, and yet there was the inescapable, undeniable likeness between her and her mother.

Suddenly the music changed, and someone called "Change partners," jarring Janet with apprehension. Mel was close to her. He had seen her, was coming toward her.

Her face froze, and instinctively, her shoulders rose. It's too soon, she thought. I'm not ready to dance yet. I won't be able to make my feet go.

At the thought of standing in the circle of his arm, the crystal shell of her new self dissolved.

When Mel stood before her, actually saying, "Will you honor me with this dance, Janny?" actually holding out his arms to her, she could do nothing but move back from him, look away from his eyes. She heard her voice croaking something stupid.

Charlie Gates lumbered past, behind her. Desperate to escape Mel's expectations, she turned and gave Charlie an elbow in the stomach.

"Well, look who's all dressed up like a lady. But you can't fool old Charlie." Breathing whiskey and high spirits, he twisted her arm in their old routine.

Janet closed her eyes to Mel and, full of self-loathing, sought the comforting familiarity of her old self. "Charlie, I'm gonna clean you out."

Mary Pat turned away from the conversation beside her to watch Mel and Janet. My, that's a good-looking

103

man I've got there, she thought. And Janet looks awful nice tonight. Probably as pretty right now as she'll ever be in her life. She's got her youth going for her, and goodness knows that won't last long, especially when the babies start coming. Yellow's a good color for her. I think I was right, doing mutton sleeves on that dress. I wonder why she's not dancing with him?

She watched, puzzled, while Mel dropped his arms and moved away from Janet. Janet was scuffling with Charlie Gates, and her voice could be heard clear across the room.

Darn that kid, anyway, Mary Pat thought. What's the matter with her, horsing around like that? She's worse than Will Junior. Here I work for a week on that dress, and what does she do? She wrestles with the black-smith.

Under her green silk lap Mary Pat felt the baby stirring. In the thrill of fright the baby's movements always gave her, she forgot Janet Borofen.

Mel elbowed his way to the end of the room where the bar stood buried in men, six deep.

"Fire and fall back, boys. Make room for the man behind," sang Alf Trumble from behind the bar. "How do, Mel. How about a little tanglefoot for you? You better fortify yourself against them gals. Fire and fall back, boys. Make room for the man behind."

His eyes watering at the strength of the whiskey,

Mel moved away from the bar. He stood tall and easy in his good clothes, pleasantly aware of how he looked. He was in his element at last, after months of work clothes and evenings at home.

His eyes wandered from face to face around the room, looking for no one in particular but reveling in the number of faces that he could put names to. This is really my town, he thought. Much more than Muscatine ever was. It's even more my town than it is Willard's. I'm young. I'll be here after he's gone, and I'll be somebody important in Eden City. Poor Mary Pat. It's a shame she can't dance tonight, as much as she loves to. Oh well, there'll be other dances, when this gets to be a real city. And she has a good time watching.

His thoughts drifted on. Wonder what got into Janny. I'd have sworn she's had a crush on me all this time, and now she won't even dance with me. Fooling around with Charlie like a darn tomboy. I guess maybe she's not as grown up as I thought she was. Looks darn near pretty, though, in that dress.

He lowered his gaze to find Miss Trumble standing before him smiling up at him across her thrashing fan. Her dress was a pile of white, draped and flounced and bunched, and quivering with the tenseness that vibrated from within it.

"Why, Mister Editor." The coyness of her words rode ridiculously on the strident voice.

Inwardly Mel flinched, but his smile was gallant.

"You look charming tonight, Miss Trumble. The party seems to be going great guns, doesn't it?"

She flapped her fan. "I was watching you dance, Melvin. I had no idea you was so light on your feet." The hard little eyes behind the fan flirted up at him with a kind of desperation.

Poor old girl, he thought. No wonder she's an old maid. She flirts with about as much subtlety as a hedge-hog. "Would you care to dance?"

The gratitude on her face depressed him.

Janet stood irresolutely against the wall. Her eyes followed Mel and Miss Trumble through the maneuvers of the Money Musk. It looked easy enough from the side-lines, and yet she was certain that her feet would have stumbled through it, probably kicking Mel and destroying any good thoughts he might have about her.

It's just as well I didn't dance with him, she thought. But what did he think when I said no? Probably thought I'd *rather* wrestle with Charlie than dance with him. Maybe he understood. No, how could he, when I don't understand, myself? How can I expect him to know I've been dreaming about it—his arm around me. . . . *Why* didn't I dance with him? I wanted to, so bad, and now he won't ask me again. Dumb, dumb, dumb.

Every time the fiddler paused, two or three men, whoever was near, asked her to dance. She accepted only Will Junior, who talked her into showing him how. In the darkest part of the dance floor she gave him a half-hearted lesson in which hand goes on the girl's back and which is held out. Gazing over his shoulder as she pushed him through the one step she knew, her eyes met Mel's for an instant, then lost him in the crowd.

She longed to be young again, free to run up and down the staircase in the lobby, as the small children were doing; or else, to be old, like Ma, and able to sit, placid and unhurtable, with the other wives. She longed to be at the soddy, where she could be herself, where no one could hurt her.

While the party was still in full cry, Janet slipped out and scuffed across the square toward home. The silk hem trailed unnoticed on the frozen ground. The icy wind came in around her shawl and found her bare throat. Her hair blew unseen across her eyes. Savagely she kicked a clump of grass.

Chapter Seven

Winter came, bringing little snow but day after day of near-zero weather. Game became scarce, and fuel precious. Christmas provided only a short-lived break in the dreariness. Often now, the Indians came into town to trade a deer carcass for a hog, which helped to relieve the monotony of winter food for both Indians and whites.

Janet spent listless hours beside the fireplace with the rest of the family, keeping at least one side of herself warm and poking at endless squares of quilting with her embroidery needle. It was too cold to stay for any length of time in the soddy, and there was little to do anywhere else in town. With the river frozen, the mill was shut down, so she didn't even have that social standby to relieve the dragging days.

When her family became too much for her to bear, she bundled up and walked back to visit Mary Pat. But somehow Mary Pat's effusive welcomes, her obvious hunger for company, had a depressing effect on Janet. It wasn't so bad on the days Mel was home, but she never knew when he would be there. As Mary Pat's delivery time drew nearer, her terror began to show through in even the lightest conversations. It set Janet's nerves on edge. One night she dreamed that Mary Pat did die, and that she and Mel grinned at each other across the grave. The dream depressed her for days.

On a particularly gloomy afternoon in early March, Vesta and Janet sat near the fire with a washtub on the floor between their feet. At one side of the tub was a gradually diminishing heap of ear corn; on the other, a slowly growing pile of cobs. While Janet grated the ears against her corn-piggin, Vesta scooped the resulting meal out of the tub with a sieve and swished out the hulls. It was a job Janet disliked, but with the mill shut down and their mill-ground meal just about gone, it was a necessary chore.

The room was silent except for the scraping and sieving, the snap of the fire, the two women breathing. It was no longer a public dining room, since the road ranch quit taking in lodgers. One of the long tables remained for the family's use, but with the second table gone, there was ample sitting room around the fireplace, and Vesta had more room for her cooking things around the kitchen corner. The beginning of a braided rug covered the floor in the bare middle of the room, its unfinished braid leaving the oval to wander across the floor to the corner where Vesta's ball of rag strips was stashed, out of the way of traffic. Despite the cheerful colors of the rug and the comfort of the fire, the room was overcast with a metallic grayness that came in through the windows, through the cracks in the walls, and under the door. The sky outside was leaden.

Janet picked up another ear of corn, slapped it against the piggin, and held it there with the flat of her hand while she rode down hard against it. The piggin-pail's metal bottom, roughened by nail holes, shredded the pebble-hard kernels into a coarse meal. It shredded bits of her skin in with the corn, too, when she was careless. Push down, turn the ear; push down, turn the ear. She tossed the naked cob aside and turned her palm toward the firelight for a close look at it. It was covered with white flakes of skin scrapings and tiny red nicks.

Fine thing, she grumbled silently. All fall I wear gloves to get my hands nice and soft, so now they're so darned soft the piggin's tearing the skin off them.

She took the little pail from between her knees and held it out to Vesta. "Want to trade jobs a while, Ma?"

Vesta went on swishing her sieve. "You go ahead there. You're doing fine. I got my rhythm going now."

Sighing, Janet picked up another ear and bore down on it. It won't be long now till I'm out there at Mel's cabin, she thought, living with them, all day, every day. He'll see my hands like this. Maybe I'll be passing him a plate or something, and he'll touch my hand and it'll feel like a darned milkweed pod. Seems like Mary Pat always stays soft-looking, no matter what she does. We're just different kinds of people, I guess, her and me. And it's her kind of woman that gets the men like Mel, the men that's worth having. When is it going to be my turn? This summer? Is my man going to come riding through this summer? Maybe he already came and I didn't know it. How do you *know* which one to marry?

How do you know? She longed, suddenly for someone she could ask, someone who would tell her the secret, simplify it for her. There'd been a time last summer when she had felt close enough to Mary Pat to have asked a question like that, but now Mary Pat was so involved with the coming baby that she had no interest in anything else. None of the other women around town was approachable about anything this personal. And Ma . . .

Janet glanced up at her mother's face, indistinct in the harsh fire-shadow. Ma was no help. Still, maybe this once she'd say something that would at least be a hint.

"Ma . . ."

There was no response. Janet wondered if she might be dozing with her eyes open and her hand automatically working the sieve.

"Ma?"

"You don't need to keep calling my name when you can see I'm setting right here. Go ahead and talk if you've got something to say."

It would have been easier to drop the whole thing, but the need to talk and be understood was heavy inside Janet. Looking at the impassive bulk of her mother, at the face whose features were so much like her own, she couldn't believe that, somewhere inside Vesta, there was not at least a little understanding.

"I was just thinking. About marriage. It's awful important to pick the right man, isn't it? I mean, whatever kind of man you marry, won't you turn out to be more or less that same kind of person yourself? Ouch." She dropped the ear she'd been grating, and sucked the bleeding heel of her hand.

Vesta answered with brusque discomfort, her eyes averted. "Don't talk foolish, girl. It don't matter much one way or the other what kind of man you marry, so long as he's decent. You got to have a home and children, and marryin's the only way to get them. But one man's about the same as another, so long as he makes a home for you."

Janet stopped working and stared for a long quiet moment at her mother. "Was that the way you felt about Pa when you married him?"

"That ain't your business." The silence built its wall between them again.

After a long time Vesta said, "If you ask me, I'd say you should have took that Mr. Kane, that come through here last summer. He was a steady-seeming fellow, and I think he took a liking to you. If you'd been a little nice to him, you could have had your own place by now, and a family on the way."

112

"Oh, Ma!" In her frustration she flung down the piggin and stamped toward the door. Why does she have to be so stupid? Janet fumed. Doesn't she have any feelings? Doesn't she have any love for me at all?

Suddenly the door flew open and Mel was there. "Come on, Janet, Vesta. It's Mary Pat's time. I'm going down to Corning for the doc. Could you hurry on out there? She doesn't want to be alone."

Janet ran into her room, her heart pounding with sudden dread. She ripped down the buffalo robe that covered the outside wall in winter. Into it she wrapped her nightgown, hairbrush, and clean shift. Then, with the afghan shawl around her shoulders and the shaggy buffalo robe rolled under her arm, she started down the timber footpath. Vesta had been placidly wrapping a ham and a pan of fresh corn bread, but Janet couldn't wait.

What if Mary Pat does die? What if she's already started having the baby when I get there, and I do something wrong? Maybe it's too late already.

She began to run.

Muffin and Jason were playing quietly on the hearth when she got there. Mary Pat was lying across the bed in the back room, dressed but with her shoes off. She turned toward Janet and half sat up, arms outstretched, tears streaming down her face. Alarmed, Janet dropped her bundle and held the weeping woman.

"There now, there now. Does it hurt that bad?" She patted the heaving shoulder blades.

"It's not hurting right now. It's just that—I don't want to die! I don't want to leave Muffy and Jasey, and I don't want this baby! Help me, Janny."

The door creaked behind her, and two small heads peered through. The children stared at Mary Pat, then at Janet, their eyes black with fear. Gently she loosened Mary Pat's grip and got up.

"You just lie back and relax a minute while I go talk to the kids."

Mary Pat clutched at her and begged with reddened eyes not to be left alone. For an instant Janet hesitated. Then she set Mary Pat back against the bed and turned to the children. She shooed them back to the chair by the fire and took Jason on her lap while Muffin pressed close against her leg.

"Is Ma going to die, Janny? Like the calf, last summer?"

Their small faces, turned up to her with fear, filled her with a sudden sureness. She pulled them in close and whispered, "No, your ma's not going to do any such thing. I promise. But right now she has a bad stomachache. Remember last fall, Jason, when you ate all those hackberries and had such a stomachache?" They all laughed a little. "You felt like you were about to die there for a while, as I recall, and you were pretty noisy about it. And here you are, bigger than ever and almost as big as Muffy, aren't you? When your ma's stomachache goes away, God's going to leave her a little baby to

114

make up for it. You used to be a little baby, Muff, no bigger than that."

The children stared in awe at the smallness of the span she measured with her hands, and when Vesta came in a little later, they were asking fascinated questions about the baby God was bringing them.

The hours that followed were endless. When the doctor came, he scolded Mary Pat for being such a sissy. He and Vesta did what little there was to be done behind the closed bedroom door, while Janet and Mel sat by the fire with a sleepy child in each lap and listened intently to the sounds from the bedroom. After a while Janet set out the ham and corn bread, and everyone ate.

During the evening the muffled groans grew more frequent. Now and then they became screams that sent Muffin and Jason running for a reassuring pair of arms. It was around midnight when Mary Pat's cries were joined by a high thin wail. Janet and Mel looked at each other. Janet smiled, and Mel let out a breath he felt he'd been holding for months.

The doctor came out of the bedroom and motioned Mel to go on in.

"Is everything all right?" Janet whispered. The sudden quiet in there alarmed her.

"Fine as rain. They got a pretty little girl. But, my, that woman carries on like she was giving birth to a two-headed ox. Easiest delivery I ever saw. All that fuss and commotion, she ought to be paddled."

During the days that followed, Janet lived more intensely than she had ever lived before. James and the dreamworld of the soddy were replaced by the fulfilling reality of Mel and his home. She slept on the floor near the fire, with two feather beds under her and two on top, and her shaggy old buffalo robe over the whole pile. Muffin and Jason and Molasses, the nearly grown pup, curled together in their bunk a few feet away. The baby's cradle was beside the fire, too, at Janet's feet.

She was the first one up in the morning, partly out of a zest for the coming day and partly out of fear of Mel's seeing her in her nightgown. By the time he emerged from the back room, Janet was dressed and combed and stirring up corn-dodger batter at the stove.

The first day or so, she tensed at each new job that confronted her, cooking a full meal alone, handling the baby, settling fights between Muffin and Jason. But as the days fell into their rhythm, as she found herself able to cope with each job, she relaxed and began to enjoy herself.

Mary Pat luxuriated in the chance to stay in bed all day. As soon as she realized that neither she nor the baby was about to die, she became almost giddy. She sat up in bed, cheerfully demanding that the baby be brought in or taken away, that Muffin come and keep her company, that they have a party on the bed.

Mel was gone most of the day. He was doing some plastering in two of the new frame houses in town on the days when the newspaper didn't need his attention.

116

When he was out of the house, Janet concentrated on caring for Mary Pat and the children. There was an atmosphere of escape from routine that was felt and relished by all of them.

But when Mel was home, it was different. The gaiety was still there, but, for Janet at least, it was underlaid with tension. Never for the smallest instant was she unaware of him. In the tiny cabin he seemed huge. She heard him breathe, across the room. She was aware, every minute, of her own actions and the loudness of her voice when she forgot to guard against it.

One morning after breakfast she sat down beside the table to do the children's hair. Muffin sat on the floor between Janet's knees, and Jason sat in front of Muffy. While Janet worked her fingers through Muffin's hair, deftly searching out the nits and drowning them in a pan of water on the table, Muffin did the same for her brother. Mel sat across the table watching them as he had his after-breakfast smoke.

"If Janet does Muff," Jason piped, "and Muff does me, who's going to do Janet?"

"Janet's a big lady. She don't need anybody to do her," Muffin said.

Smiling, Janet glanced across the table at Mel. He was staring at her with an odd, bemused look, as though he were wondering who she was. Her heart fluttered as their eyes held. She looked away.

When the baby was four days old, Mary Pat wrapped

a quilt around her shoulders and joined the family for dinner. Janet joked with her and made an elaborate fuss over serving the guest of honor, but beneath her gaiety she found herself almost resenting Mary Pat's presence among them. After that day it wasn't quite as much fun as it had been, serving Mel his meals, taking care of his children.

On the last night of Janet's stay, they had a thank-you party. Muffin and Jason were put to bed in the back room, while Janet, Mel, and Mary Pat sat near the fire and celebrated with dried apple pie and just a little of Mel's good wine. The baby woke, and Mary Pat reached down to rock the cradle.

Janet glanced from her to Mel. He was watching his wife and smiling a little over his mug of wine. "Aren't you sorry you made such a fuss?" he teased.

Mary Pat turned to look blankly at him. "What are you talking about?"

"The baby. All that fuss you made about dying, screaming and crying and scaring the stuffing out of the kids."

Janet grinned at his teasing tone, but the humor escaped Mary Pat.

"Listen, Mel Makinich, you just try having a baby sometime. It's the worst agony in the world. You wouldn't be so darn brave, either . . ."

While she ranted, gathering steam and outrage, Mel's eyes met Janet's. He smiled quietly, as though they shared a secret tolerance of Mary Pat's moods. His eyes held hers for an instant after his smile died. In the moving shadows of the firelight Janet flushed. She was glad for the dimness of the room, glad he couldn't read her face.

". . . ask any woman, Mel. They all scream a little. I'm not the only one." Mary Pat's tirade spent itself.

Mel said lightly, "I bet Janet wouldn't have been such a sissy." Again their eyes met, but only for an instant.

Mary Pat looked from Mel to Janet and blazed, "Well, if Janet's so darn wonderful . . ." She searched for words, then suddenly let the subject drop.

Janet cleared her throat and toyed with the crumbs of pie on her plate. It wasn't long before Mary Pat's irritation disappeared, but the aftertaste of it stayed with Janet long after everyone was in bed. She lay on her pallet and saw Mel's eyes burning into hers, heard Mary Pat's bitter words echoing in the darkness around her. She felt an overwhelming relief that she was going home tomorrow, and a vague sort of shame, as though she had betrayed a friend. Silently she pleaded, But I never wanted *him,* Mary Pat. Just—somebody *like* him.

Chapter Eight

"Anything else for you, Janet?" Virgie Wheelock asked from behind the counter.

"No, that's all." Janet paid for the lamp wicks and smiled at Virgie. It still felt odd to be buying things in a store, instead of selling them, although it had been three months now since Pa's store had relinquished its hardware business to the Wheelocks and begun specializing in soft goods and groceries only. Wheelock Hardware, Seed, and Harness had outgrown its original structure, the de-wheeled covered wagon, and was now housed in a blocky wood-and-tar-paper building down the street from the hotel. The family lived in the back room, and Virgie, youthful in spite of her toothlessness, minded the store and her several small children, while Mr. Wheelock worked at the mill.

Janet left the store and started up the plank walk toward home. It was late March, and the town square was a saturated sponge under its cover of dried prairie grass. Not even Janet cut across it during the muddy season. At the corner by the hotel, she gathered her skirt and made her way across Adams Street on the stepping-stones made from slices of tree trunks. She was still watching her step when she landed on the other side, and she nearly collided with Jay Zupin.

"Afternoon, Jay."

"Ah, Miss B, you're looking charming today, mighty charming. Won't you step over to the hotel with me for a glass of cider, and brighten an old bachelor's day?"

She looked down at him suspiciously, even while she allowed herself to be steered back across the stepping logs and into the hotel bar. Jay Zupin didn't throw around compliments and drinks unless he wanted something, but there was nothing waiting for her at home but work. She settled herself at one of the tables in the dining room and tried not to let the room, and its memories of the dance party, darken the afternoon.

"This is by way of a celebration," Jay said as he raised his whiskey glass to Janet's mug of cider. "I want you to be the first to know. I've just managed to buy another hundred acres of government land south and west of the square. Going to get it surveyed into streets and building lots and start selling them off right away. It's going to be Eden City's finest residential section."

Willard's Ford, Janet said silently. But in spite of his irritating pushiness, she had begun to like this sleek little man with his unflagging belief in the town and his clean, spicy smell. She wondered, sometimes, why he wasn't married. Every once in a while she thought she saw, beneath his energy and eloquence, a rather wistful knowledge that he was an outsider, not a permanent resident of anyplace.

"Why don't you stay here?" she said suddenly. "I mean permanently, even after you get the town going."

He looked startled, softened, almost visibly gratified. But his voice was as brisk as ever. "Because a city planner has to go where he's needed. It's my profession. No use for me in a town that's established and thriving."

Before she could answer, Alf Trumble came out from behind the bar and stood over their table. "Everything okay here, folks? How are you, Janet?"

"Fine, thanks."

"Usual number for the meeting tonight?" he said to Jay. Jay nodded, and then the men talked for a few minutes about the coming town meeting. As she listened, Janet found herself wishing they hadn't begun holding the meetings in the hotel bar, where women and children were discouraged from coming at night. She missed the meetings, seeing the men all shaved and combed, seeing Mel in his paisley vest standing up to give his committee reports.

When Mr. Trumble left, Jay leaned across the table and said, in a quieter voice than usual, "Janet dear, I wanted to ask a favor of you."

I knew it, she thought. Oh well, it was a free cider, anyway. "What?"

122

He sat back, sighed, looked at her with fondness in his small bright eyes. "It's that stubborn father of yours, still holding out for naming the town Willard's Ford. Hell, pardon—heck, Miss B, the other folks in this town don't really care about the name, they just enjoy a fight, and as long as your pa keeps up his selfish attitude, some of the rest of them's going to back him up just out of orneriness. We can't get a post office till we settle on a name, and it won't be a real town until it has that post office. Now I know Willard Borofen just dotes on you, Janet. Yes sir, dotes on you. If you'd just put in a word —it means a lot to me."

He seemed so genuinely concerned that she found it hard to get mad at him for trying to use her. She gave him a direct look and said, "He don't dote on me; he dotes on Will Junior. He wouldn't pay a bit of attention to anything I said, and even if he did, I'm on his side, Jay, not yours. But thanks for the cider anyhow."

He gave her a long searching look, then, with a compressed smile, raised his glass to her. "I spoke out of turn, Miss B, and I beg pardon. Will you walk along with me upstairs to the *Clarion* office? I want to give Mel these new lithographs to send out with his back-east editions."

He spread the new lithographs out on the table, and ordered another round of drinks.

On the first afternoon that was both warm and dry, Janet slipped out of the house with the petticoat kindling sack under her arm. She waited until everyone was out of sight so no one would ask what she intended to gather in the sack, because she hadn't been able to think of a believable lie. It was too early in the year for nuts, and too late in the day for kindling.

She took the faint, neglected path behind the outhouse until she was out of sight of the house, then angled off through the timber in the general direction of the soddy. Today she felt a need to stay away from any regular path where she might meet someone. The ground underfoot was spongy with spring rains and last year's oak leaves. It was covered with ferns and soft moss and blankets of violets.

At the creek she turned and followed its banks out into the sun. Pausing at the edge of the timber, she looked slowly around her. Behind her was the dark shelter of the woods. In front and on both sides, rolling swells of pale green. The town was out of sight. Mel's cabin, a mile or so straight ahead, was hidden by the low hills, but she could make out a line of smoke from the cabin's chimney, rising straight up through the gentle air.

The grass she walked over was short and fine beneath its covering of last year's stalks. It was laced with the tiny pastel wild flowers that can survive only while the prairie grass is at its shortest.

When she got to the clearing in front of the soddy, she dropped the sack and, bracing herself for the sight, opened the door. It was worse than she'd expected. Mud, washed down through the winter and early spring, lay six inches deep over everything. The table top wore its mud like cake frosting. The buffalo robe lay in a heap on the floor, dragged down from its pegs by the weight of its soggy fur. The grass roots that hung from the ceiling were inches longer this year, because of the mud that had washed away from them and down into the soddy. Moisture was still dripping from the roots, even though it hadn't rained for days.

Dismayed at the job ahead of her, Janet slogged once around the tiny room, then went back outside. I'll have to figure out some kind of a scoop, she decided. I won't even worry about that today, though. I'll do the stomach instead.

In the center of the clearing the cottonwoods allowed a small beam of sun to reach the ground. Here she brought the sack and opened it. First she took out the braid ring, then a little bottle of glycerin and rose water that she'd taken from the store with Willard's absent-minded permission. It was a delicate white glass bottle with a ring of tiny roses on the front, the sort of bottle Del or Mary Pat would feel at home with. Janet cradled it in her hands and tried not to see the contrast between the bottle and the coarse, big-boned hands that held it.

She set the bottle down in the grass and pulled from the sack her yellow silk dress. It was crumpled from months of burial in the bottom of her storage chest. She shook it out and spread it carefully atop a clump of sumac, then stepped back to look at it.

It didn't hurt nearly so much any more, she realized. At first, after the dance party, the sight of it hanging on the peg in her room had depressed her so much that she'd stuffed it in the chest under her summer shift. Then, it had taunted her with her failure. Now, lying there on the sumac bush by her soddy, the dress seemed to belong to this world, as she did. Out here, away from Miss Trumble, Will and her father, and even Mel; away from her mother, whose physical resemblance to Janet seemed sometimes like a shadow of doom to the part of her that was struggling to come to life; out here in the soddy's protective solitude she was strong enough to wear a yellow silk dress without feeling foolish in it.

She longed to put it on for a while, to imagine what James would think of the dress if he were real. But there was work to do. From the depths of the kindling sack she dumped a packet of hay tied with rawhide thongs. She undid the thongs and shook the hay away. In the center of the packet was the membranous covering from the stomach of the sheep Willard had butchered that morning. Smiling, she held it up to the sun to admire its undamaged wholeness. Yes, this would do fine. With a wad of hay for a scrubber and the creek for a washtub, she cleaned the transparent sack inside and out. Long after the last trace of fat had disappeared, she rubbed and swished it through the cold creek water.

Finally she shook it out and spread it on the grass in the spot of sun.

Whistling softly between her teeth, she found a short, heavy stick and went inside the house to begin scraping the mud off the table top and the shelf. Every now and then she left her work to go outside and shift the stomach sack as the sunny spot moved east. By the time the table and shelf were scraped and washed clean, the sack was dry and sweet smelling. With one of the rawhide thongs she tied off the hole in the bottom of the membrane sack and, by tearing carefully, widened the top opening.

"There now, that should keep the mud off," she said, laying the sack lightly on the bush beside the yellow silk. Then she took the dress down and folded it as neatly as she could, smoothing wrinkles as she went, until it was small enough to be jammed into the sack. Carefully she tucked the ring in among the folds.

Inside the soddy Janet started to lay the dress package on the shelf beside her work gloves and the glycerin and rose water bottle, but it didn't seem right there. The dress should be someplace more secure, less vulnerable in case anyone should happen by and find the soddy. She turned slowly, searching the dimness. Nothing there but the table and chair, the empty broken slats of the corner bunk, the dangling stovepipe.

The stovepipe. Stooping low beneath it, she squinted up into the pipe. No glimmer of blue sky showed through. She reached up through the pipe until her fingers confirmed the fact that the pipe was mashed flat somewhere above.

"Perfect."

She knocked out a rain of loose dirt and flecks of rust with her broom handle, then cautiously worked the dress packet up into the pipe. Her cleverness made her feel smug, and she began to whistle again.

Through the spring and early summer no one in Willard's Ford was enough aware of Janet's growing pre-occupation to comment on it. Vesta watched her daughter through sleepy eyes and wondered now and then what Janet found to do out there in the timber every afternoon. But as long as she was home in time to help with supper, it didn't much matter.

Will Junior had more important things on his mind than Janet's comings and goings. New stores were going up on the square, and half a dozen houses were in various stages of fascinating construction. There were one or two new boys who had moved to town, and an occasional girl for whom he raced his bald-faced horse down Adams Street and over the log stepping-stones. The activity at the mill was at an all-time high now, too, with all the lumber the home-builders needed.

It seemed to Willard, when he thought about it, that Janet was off by herself a lot these days. The thought crossed his mind that she might be meeting a man out there in the timber. But the possibility only made him snort to himself and shake his head.

Mel noticed that Janet didn't seem to be hanging around quite as much as she used to, but when he did see her, she was as friendly as ever—in fact, sometimes she smiled at him in a way that made him a little uncomfortable—so he wasn't worried that she was angry with him for any reason. And with both the local and the back-east editions of the *Clarion* demanding his time, along with the work of keeping up his cornfield at home, he had little time to wonder what Janet Borofen was doing with her afternoons.

Mary Pat saw no change in Janet. The baby was a constant care, and Jason was taking out his jealousy of his new sister by wandering off more and more frequently. Janet often stopped in for a visit late in the afternoons, but if she acted differently, Mary Pat failed to notice.

As the weeks passed, the game Janet played at the sod house began to take on a reality that gradually overshadowed the other part of her life. James, whom she had made up just for the fun of it or perhaps in an effort to keep her daydreaming separate from Mel, was becoming alarmingly real. She seldom thought about him except when she was at the soddy, but he seemed to wait for her on the summer afternoons just within the shadows of the hut.

As a child, she had never had time for playing house, not with Pa there, laughing with pride when she rode or shot well or put out a successful string of prairie-chicken traps. Now, the solitude of the soddy allowed her to play the role of herself in fulfillment, like a little girl playing house. She did it instinctively, aware that she was being silly, wasting the summer sitting around the abandoned soddy in a yellow silk dress, talking to imaginary people. But she knew, too, that it was the right thing to do. The softness of her untried womanhood was growing larger and stronger, in the protection of the soddy. When she talked with James, there was nothing to be afraid of; he never sneered or acted superior. With him, she dared to use better grammar than was used around the Borofen house.

"There was a lovely poem in this week's *Clarion*," she said one day. "Have you read it yet?" She was seated at the little table by the window, wrapped in yellow silk and the scent of glycerin and rose water. Her hair was still damp from her bath in the creek. The braid ring gleamed on her finger.

"I'll read it for you. It's one of Mr. Wordsworth's. I was discussing it with Mel Makinich—the editor of the paper, you know. He's an old friend of mine. I'll let you in on a little secret. I believe he meant for this poem to be dedicated to me; he's been secretly in love with me for a long time. I hope you're not jealous." She laughed, and picked up the *Clarion* she'd brought out to the soddy earlier.

"It goes like this, James.

She was a Phantom of delight
When first she gleamed upon my sight;
A lovely Apparition, sent
To be a moment's ornament;

An apparition is a ghost, James."

She moved toward the doorway to catch the sun, then followed its warmth out into the clearing as she read on.

" . . . I saw her upon nearer view,
A Spirit, yet a Woman too!
Her household motions light and free,
And steps of virgin-liberty . . ."

While she read, she could feel the lightness and freedom, the virgin liberty of her movements around the clearing. "Wasn't that lovely, James? Did you understand all of it?"

She turned back toward the soddy, but the warm sun felt so good on her damp hair that she didn't go inside. Instead, she ran around past the door and up to the top of the hill that made the soddy's roof. Looking east, into the great grassy empty waves of prairie, she shouted, "Darn you, James, or whoever you are, why don't you hurry up and *get* here? I'm ready for you!"

Then, aware that she could be seen from Mel's cornfield, she ran back down again.

Willard pushed his chair back from the dinner table and belched as quietly as possible. Janet had already disappeared for the afternoon, and Will Junior was gone for the day, helping deliver lumber to construction sites for Carl Morton.

It was the first steaming-hot day of the summer. The room was bright and quiet except for the eternal humming of the flies around the table and the creak of the floorboards as Vesta carried dishes to the washbasin.

He felt like talking to someone, even to Vesta. "Well, tomorrow night should settle it, one way or the other."

She glanced over her shoulder at him with a look that asked what he was talking about.

"The meeting tomorrow night," he answered. "The final, once-and-for-all vote on the name. It has to be final this time, so we can file the post office application."

She turned back to her dishes. "Lot of foolishness, if you ask me. It's a plumb vanity, wanting a town named after you."

"Ahh." With a wave of his hand toward her back, he dismissed her. If she didn't understand him any better than that after all these years . . .

"Are them boys racing out there again?" she asked as the beats of a galloping horse grew loud outside.

The store door opened, and Bob Crow ran, panting, into the Borofen sitting room. "Mr. Borofen, big news! I was just down to the hotel, and there's a man down

132

there, just come in from Kansas Territory. Says they found gold out there." He paused to catch his breath. "Some place called Cherry Creek, way yonder on the far side of Kansas. Says it's a bigger strike than the California one. Man, Billy and I are heading out there just as quick as we can!"

The creek in front of the soddy wasn't deep enough for swimming, but it was fine for bathing if one was careful about stirring up the mud along the bank. Janet waded up out of it, clutching her soap chunk and stepping high and wide over the bank and up to the grass. With handfuls of water scooped from the barrel well, she rinsed off her feet.

"There now, clean as a hound's tooth, from top to bottom."

She spread her old gray-brown homespun on the grass where the sun came through, and sat down on it to dry. She felt oddly excited today, as though the air were charged with a mysterious tension that blew into her, through her drying skin, on the hot afternoon wind. Maybe it's the way the clearing looks today, she thought, as if it's covered with snow in the middle of June.

The cottonwood trees that arched over the clearing were in full shed. The ground was covered with their white cotton-fluff, and with every gust of the strong hot wind the blizzard was renewed. Cotton clung to the wet strands of Janet's hair, her damp bare back and shoulders.

She hardly noticed. There was a yearning in her today that made her want to run out and find her future, drag it from wherever it was hiding, shake it out and put it on. She felt ready; she felt the frustration of readiness that lacks a challenge.

A bit of cottonwood fuzz drifted past her face. With it came a memory—an autumn afternoon, a milkweed pod spilling itself to the wind, Mel. The yellow dress had been just bits and pieces then, untested. Now it was familiar, comfortable, ready to be tested again. But there was no one here. Melancholy brushed her.

The wind and the sun had dried her now, except for the thick back part of her hair. She rubbed herself all over with glycerin and rose water, then got up and pulled on her shift and the yellow dress. It had been airing on the sumac bush while she bathed, so now it smelled of the sun, and fell away with almost no wrinkles when she dropped it over her head. With the sudden lift of spirits that always came when she put the dress on, she kicked the old homespun out of the middle of her clearing. It landed against a tree trunk and lay there in a heap.

I need some flowers today, she thought, running around to the top of the soddy where the sunflowers were already nearly waist high. No, not sunflowers. They're too big.

She found a tangle of daisies, picked two of the smallest blooms, and worked their stems through the top buttonhole of her dress. The stems scratched, but the little blossoms were necessary to her mood. Up here, the wind blew stronger and more steadily, coming, as her man would come, from the east. She turned to face full into it. It lifted her hair from her shoulders and plastered her body with yellow silk. It brought the smell of plowed ground and wild flowers.

When she opened her eyes, she realized that Mel was in his cornfield, hoeing along in her direction. She knew she'd better get down before he saw her. But she stayed another minute, another minute or two before she turned and ran down to the safety of the clearing.

She felt giddy. The tension inside her demanded release. She laughed and did a self-conscious whirl across the clearing. When she closed her eyes, the clearing became the hotel ballroom, and the wind in the trees was music. She raised her arms, threw back her head, and smiled up into James's face.

> *"Greensleeves was all my joy,*
> *Greensleeves was my delight,*
> *Greensleeves was my heart of gold,*
> *And who but my Lady Greensleeves?"*

They swayed across the ballroom, Janet and James, in perfect time with the music they sang together.

> *"Greensleeves was all my joy,*
> *Greensleeves was my delight . . ."*

When she opened her eyes and saw Mel standing at the edge of the clearing, her heart turned over. She froze, her arms still raised around her partner, who faded before the reality of Mel.

His face was grave; his eyes clung to hers.

Suddenly she was sure and powerful. She smiled a soft smile and went on singing. "Greensleeves was my heart of gold, and who but my Lady Greensleeves?"

The wind blew him to her and set them in motion. They hummed and whirled gravely, compressing their joy. Her bare feet followed his work boots over the grass, stirring clouds of cotton that rose and billowed around them. Janet saw the sky revolve behind Mel's head, felt the pressure of his hand against her back, guiding her. There was no resistance in her.

The sky ceased revolving. They stood.

Mel's face, so close to hers, wore an expression of wonder, of discovery. His gaze darted from one of her eyes to the other, back and forth, and finally dropped to her lips. She caught her breath.

He brushed a feather-light kiss on her forehead, then turned and disappeared around the soddy.

Chapter Nine

At supper that night, the talk was all of the Cherry Creek gold strike. The news penetrated Janet's consciousness only faintly. The fact that some stranger hundreds of miles away had found gold had nothing to do with her life. It was nothing compared to what had just happened out at the soddy. Still, as the meal progressed, she became aware that Pa was disturbed, more disturbed than he'd ever been before, that she could remember.

The conversation didn't really catch her attention, though, until Will Junior said he guessed he'd go tell the Makiniches about the gold strike after supper.

"No," Janet said, louder than she meant to. "I'll go. I want to tell them."

The strong winds of the afternoon had blown the sky full of thunderclouds by the time she tossed the dishwater out the back door and started for Mel's cabin. She took the shortcut behind the outhouse and through the timber. The sky was lavender-gray and low, and the first far-off rumbles sounded around her.

But she was oblivious to the evening. All she saw was the golden afternoon, the look in Mel's eyes. The feeling of power was still with her, warming her. She knew, now, that she could make a man like Mel look at her with reverence. Del's marriage seemed a minor accomplishment by comparison.

And if Mel could look at her that way, then someday, when her man came down the trail, he might look at her that way too, and see what Mel saw, and value her.

She felt oddly independent of Mel Makinich as she crossed the open stretch of prairie toward his cabin. It was almost as though, having fulfilled his purpose, he had become less necessary.

The sky's lavender cast was over the grass now, making the landscape a subtle monotone relieved only by the light of Mel's cabin. The door was closed against the rising wind, but lamplight poured out the windows. As she approached, Janet saw Mel and Mary Pat through the front window. They were seated at the table, with their empty plates between them. Mel was leaning back in his chair rolling his after-supper cigarette, and Mary Pat was nursing the baby.

I'll wait a little before I knock, she thought. Mary Pat might be embarrassed if I barge in while she's nursing the baby.

She sat down against the wall to wait for the sound

138

of Mary Pat putting the baby to bed. Their voices came to her plainly through the open window. Janet listened first with mild interest, then with sudden tension.

". . . just dancing away out there, all by herself." It was Mel's voice, reflective, but with a note of humor at the bottom of it. "Craziest sight I ever saw. She had on that yellow dress you made for her last fall, and she'd stuck some flowers in the front. You should have seen her, Patsy; she looked like a different person."

There was a long silence while the baby fretted, then settled down again. In a bright, interested voice Mary Pat said, "Well, go on. What did you do then? Did she see you?"

"Yes, this was the strange part. I guess I kind of got caught up in the spirit of the thing. I mean, it was such an unexpected sight to see, out there at the back of nowhere. And Janny seemed so—I don't know—like she was off in another world. Before I knew it, I was down there dancing with her."

He chuckled, and Mary Pat laughed. "That's a sight I'd like to have seen."

"You know, I never realized there was a soddy over there," he said. "The old place has a perfect camouflage. We'll take a walk over there one of these days and I'll show it to you. You'll . . ."

Janet couldn't stand any more. She was on her feet, running up the hill and along Mel's road, trying to outrun the sound of his voice.

How could he tell her? How could he tell her that? she raged silently.

The betrayal swelled with each pounding step, with each heavy chilled raindrop that struck her. Once, she tripped and sprawled headlong in the grass beside the road. When she raised her head, she was face to face with one of last year's milkweeds. The pods were barren and ugly. Suddenly she remembered the tender way his hand had cupped the pod just before his thumb dug out the fluff with a quick, thoughtless motion.

Deliberately ignoring rain and mud, she lay for a long time in the grassy ditch, propped up on her elbows, shredding long blades of grass with her thumbnail. A fury of self-loathing washed through her, wave upon wave. To have exposed herself to Mel's patronage; to have dared to think some part of his loyalty might have belonged to her instead of his wife; to have assumed so much, so wrongly! She tore at the grass and called herself every kind of a fool. Her feeling of independence from him was already forgotten.

What am I going to do, next time I have to look him in the face, or Mary Pat either? she thought with an almost nauseating desperation. They're going to look at me and think about that big crazy girl dancing around out in the woods in a silk dress. They're back there right now, having a good laugh about crazy old Janet.

Through the bitterness of her thoughts came a small

sad memory of the soddy, where she had been happy, where she could never go now; the mortification would be unbearable. And she thought of the braid ring and the dress.

But I won't have any more use for silk dresses, anyway. I was only fooling myself in that dress, thinking I could be that kind of woman. I'm not, and I might as well not even try. Sensitivity! Who was he trying to fool?

Without conscious thought she got up and began walking toward home as slowly as possible. She had an overpowering need to strike out at something, to hurt, to destroy. Her muscles ached with it; her fists clenched around it.

But there was nothing to strike at, only Charlie's corn and the road and the rain that glued her clothes to her. Above her a thunderhead exploded. Lightning cracked down and struck a tree in the pasture, not far from where she walked. The crash, the smell of the burning wood, the realization that she might be hit next, drained some of the immediacy off of her tension, and left her oddly satisfied.

Two mornings later, at the breakfast table, Vesta said, "How'd the voting go last night, Willard?"

"Didn't vote." Willard's coffee mug slammed the table.

Janet came out of her private thoughts long enough

to say, "Didn't vote on the town names? I thought last night's meeting was going to be the big showdown. What happened?"

"Gold fever is what happened. It's more catchin' than the plague, and just about as good for you. Half the fool town was all set to pack up and move to Cherry Creek this morning. Just throw away all the work that's been put into Willard's Ford, trying to build up a town out of nothing, and now, just when it's beginning to look like something around here, some nugget-head yells gold, and boy, that's all they need. Vesta, what's the matter with you? Can't you see when a man's out of coffee?"

Janet stared down at the syrup-sogged johnnycake that rode on the battered ridges of her plate. It irritated her that Ma went right on using the tin plates for the family, even though the cupboard now held a handsome set of Red Wing crockery.

If anybody ever marries me, she thought, I'm going to use the nicest things I have for everyday. I wonder if very many people from here really will go to Cherry Creek. Probably not. It'd be foolish if they did. I wonder if Mel and Mary Pat would ever think about going. I wish they would. Then I wouldn't have to keep on dodging them. But they won't. Mel loves Willard's Ford every bit as much as Pa does, seems like, and he's getting such a good start here with the *Clarion*. He doesn't give two whoops in a rain barrel for gold, anyhow, just for his newspaper.

142

In the ache of thinking about Mel, she hadn't heard the conversation around her, but the sudden thunder of Pa's voice brought her back. Pa was standing, and so was Will Junior, with the table between them.

". . . from my own son!" Willard was shouting. "You ungrateful little pot-licker! I hope to hell you didn't mean that remark, because if you did, I'm going to clean you out like greased lightning passing a funeral. No son of mine is going off looking for gold." He spat out the word *gold* as though it burned his tongue; then, more calmly, he sat down. Will Junior did, too.

"You just wait and see," Willard went on. "In a month, two at the most, those Crow boys will be back here, broke and wore out and dragging their tails, and you can have the laugh on them for being smart enough to stay where you're at."

Watching her brother's face, Janet saw his rebellion begin to fade beneath his normal placid expression. He's got it too easy here, she thought. He ain't about to go off someplace where he'd have to work for his meals.

"Janet," Willard said as he rose from the table, "you stay around the store today. It'll probably be busy in there, with all these folks getting ready to leave. Will Junior and I are going to go out and try to talk some sense into these people. Jay Zupin gave them a good speech at the meeting last night, told them all the sensible reasons for staying put, but I don't think he did too much good. Maybe we can do better. Ready, son?"

Janet went down the step into the store, thinking how much nicer it would be to go and catch a horse and ride out into the prairie grass, just amble along all day by herself, and think. Instead, sighing, she pulled back the board that latched the outside door, and let the door swing open. A small crowd was already waiting; they startled her.

"Thought you was never going to open up," Billy Crow said as the crowd pushed in. "We got to get our supplies, so me and Bob can get on our way. We're going to be rich, Jan!" He picked her up and swung her once, but her weight was more than he'd figured, and one swing was as much as he could manage.

She pulled down her dress front and said, "You're crazy, Billy. Keep your hands to yourself and give me your list. When are you leaving?" She took his list and began moving around the room, gathering the items.

"Today. Quick as we can. What did your pa say about Will going with us? Is he going to let him?" Janet sent a level look over her shoulder at him, and Billy said, "That's what I thought. I told Will his pa would never let him go. Heck, our dad's even talking about maybe coming out himself, him and Ma, if us boys git lucky out there. You ought to come, Janet."

She looked at him, snorted, and began adding up the bill.

"No, now, seriously, Jan, why don't you? With all the men that's going to be out there, you could latch onto one of them before the summer's out, and if you're lucky, you might get a rich one."

For a moment she paused in her adding, then shook her head. "No. I know what I want, and the kind of man I'd want to marry'd have more sense than to go off chasing after gold. This comes to thirty-two dollars, Billy. I think you and Bob're crazy to go out there, but I sure wish you all the luck in the world. All right, who's next?"

The day flew by in a rush of business such as Janet had never seen in the Willard's Ford store. She worked as fast as she could, assembling bags of flour, slabs of side pork, and packets of tobacco, while the customers bent and strained to load their heavy sacks onto wagon beds. Her lunch was snatched on the run from the cracker and pickle barrels. Most of the customers were just traveling through Willard's Ford from the east, on their way toward Cherry Creek, but as the afternoon passed, Janet counted a disquieting number of Adams County people.

Once she looked up to see Charlie Gates watching her from the other side of the counter. She was surprised at her own intensity as she said, "Oh, Charlie, not you too."

"Not me too, what? Oh, you mean, am I fixing to go chasing gold? Nah." He laughed. "I just needed some salt, if you got any left. Looks like you been doing a land-office trade in here today."

She straightened up and brushed the hair out of her eyes with her sleeve. "I don't think even the land office could beat this, Charlie. I believe we got a little salt left, though."

She came around the counter and shoved her way through the waiting men, toward the salt bin. The heat, and the demands of the crowd, were beginning to wear her temper thin. "Move, blast it. Lady coming through." The figure blocking her way turned and became Mel.

"Sorry, Janny," he said, smiling and making way for her.

She flushed, first because of the way she'd spoken to him, then for the shame of what he must be remembering —the dancing at the soddy, laughing about it later with his wife. All day she'd been too busy to think about it, but now the memory came back as sharp as new. She turned away from him and got Charlie's salt.

By the time she got back to her counter, a strange man was there, arguing with Charlie.

"I tell you I just come from Cherry Creek," the man shouted, "and I swear on my mother's memory, that strike is the real thing. It ain't no flash in the pan. There's fortunes to be made, just strolling through them hills. It's like nothing I ever saw before in my life, man. Anybody that don't take advantage is just plain blind or crazy."

"Well *I* ain't about to go gally-vanting out there," Charlie shouted back. "Are you calling me crazy?" He flexed his knees and shoved up his shirt sleeves.

146

Janet saw his stance and the eager ring of onlookers beginning to form around the two men. "Oh no you don't," she yelled, forcing her way into the center of the storm. "Not in here with my breakables. You go on outside now, all of you."

Almost immediately the store was emptied of fighters and watchers, all except Janet and Mel, who watched through the window as Charlie began to circle and jab.

"It sure doesn't take much to set Charlie off, does it?" Mel said.

"I guess everybody's a little on edge right now."

"Well, one thing you don't need worry about," he said in a quiet voice, "the Makiniches and the *Clarion* are here to stay, even if the whole county ups and leaves." His hand rested briefly on her shoulder, but she was braced against feeling anything from it, or from the sound of his voice. She held herself silent and rigid, and in a moment the hand was gone.

"Looks like the fight's over," she said. Charlie was reaching down to help his opponent to his feet.

Mel went outside then. From the doorway Janet heard him offer to buy the man, and Charlie, a drink at the hotel, in exchange for an interview for his paper, a firsthand account of the Cherry Creek gold camp. Janet's eyes followed him as long as he was in sight; then she went back to her counter.

She felt relieved and oddly strengthened by seeing Mel again. The awkward moment was past. Thinking back on it, she realized that Mel's effect on her hadn't been as strong as it had always been before. She had stood up there beside him, with his hand on her shoulder, and it hadn't made her come completely undone, as it would have a week ago. It was as though, having been hurt by him, she was beginning to develop a resilience to his charm. She smiled with genuine warmth at the customer who waited across the counter for her attention.

By the end of the week the store's supply of flour, salt, frying pans, and side pork was running dangerously low. At suppertime she bolted the door and went to find her father.

Willard was leaning over the corral gate, staring up the road toward the square. It was still full daylight, but their two shadows reached all the way across the small enclosure. He seemed not to notice her standing beside him.

"Pa, we're just about out of supplies. Are you going to go after some more tomorrow?"

There was no answer.

"If you don't, you're going to miss out on the best run of business we ever had. Will and I have been taking in close to eight hundred dollars a day. Pa?"

He stared on. The flesh of his face hung heavily, his eyes peered out but didn't focus.

Frustrated, Janet raised her voice. "If you don't get on over to Nebraska City and get these supplies, I'm going to go myself."

Before she had time to ask herself whether she really would do such a thing, Jay Zupin's buggy pulled up beside them. Willard turned and waited for Jay to get down, but he remained in the buggy. Jay's neat little hands flexed the reins in a quick, nervous gesture. Before he spoke, Janet knew what he was going to say.

"I've about decided to take a little run out there myself, Mr. B. Just to see what all the shouting's about. I understand that country out there has a lot of natural resources. Bound to be new towns springing up. New towns springing up out there left and right in another few months, and of course, that's my profession, you know, helping new towns get off on the right foot."

He paused, but Willard said nothing. He lowered his voice and went on in a slightly calmer tone. "This is a nice spot you've got here, Willard. I've enjoyed my stay. But it's just not up-and-coming enough for a man like myself. I'll be able to do big things out there in Cherry Creek." For an instant his eyes met Janet's, and she thought she saw a suggestion of regret in his face. She forced a smile, and he smiled back, more genuinely than was usual for him.

He turned his horse around and started to drive away, then paused and called back, "I'm going to call my new project Eden City, so it might be a good idea if you stick to the name Willard's Ford. Less confusion that way." He waved his whip and drove off.

The irony of Jay's parting remark broke through Willard's mask, and he swore, softly but thoroughly, working his way through his entire list of words Vesta didn't allow in the house. Then, in a voice heavy with resignation, he said, "You better mind the store again tomorrow, sister. I've got to make a run over to Nebraska City for a load of supplies. I expect we're running a little short, aren't we?"

After supper a few days later, Janet and Will Junior walked down to the square for a look around. The stillness of the summer twilight lay with unusual weight over the deserted square. The lights from the hotel bar, and the horses tied outside it, only accented the air of desertion. Wordlessly, they ambled along the plank walk, hands in pockets, eyes moving slowly from building to building. In front of the livery stable Janet pointed to the sign tacked on its door. "Gone to Cherry Creek."

"He just got through flooring the loft," Janet murmured.

They cut across at the corner, automatically avoiding the lights of the hotel. On the saloon door, painted in crude letters, was "Gone to git rich." They paused in front of Wheelock's Hardware to talk to Virgie and her husband, who were sitting on the store's front steps.

"Looks kind of lonesome, don't it?" Virgie said. She smiled a wistful, toothless smile.

"It won't last," Janet said. "First thing you know, we'll get word that the gold strike is all played out, and these people will be coming back."

"I don't know," Mr. Wheelock said. "I'd like to think that, and Lord knows I don't want to have to move on, now we're settled in here, but a man can't make a living selling hardware in a ghost town, now can he?"

The word *ghost town* went through Janet like a chill. She turned and looked around her. The grass in the square was mowed this summer for the first time, and the paths around its sides were beginning to look like genuine streets. There were buildings on all four sides now, too. Lots of empty spaces between them, but not nearly so many as last fall. Looking south, she could see Jay Zupin's residential plots, marked with neat rows of red bunting flags. Already half a dozen houses stood facing one another from the centers of their flag-marked yards.

To the east, behind the hotel, Janet could see several carelessly scattered tar-paper shacks and soddies. Definite footpaths connected them, and most had small lilac bushes and young fruit trees planted around them. They seemed so familiar to her now, so settled in and permanent, that she couldn't remember what the prairie had looked like before they were there.

"Come on," Will Junior said suddenly. "We better get home." He ran across the square ahead of her and sent a series of loud Indian whoops into the air. But the sound of his yelling couldn't quite drown out, in Janet's mind, the soft whisper of "ghost town."

I just can't get over it, she thought, walking slowly

and staring around her. One day it's practically a boom-town, new buildinges going up faster than weeds in a cornfield. And the next day it's going the other direction.

From the scaffolding of a half-completed ware-house, a rope swung lazily in the rising night wind. It's just like that rope, she thought, first going one way and then the other, but you don't ever see when it changes direction. See, Mel? I can have fancy thoughts even when I'm not doing it to impress you.

She felt pleased with herself, and relieved to find that it wasn't really vital to her happiness whether Willard's Ford survived or not.

Chapter Ten

It was early August, five weeks after the Cherry Creek gold strike. Mel sat in his office with his back to the desk and his feet braced against the low windowsill. The heat blew in from outside and washed over him in waves. Flies filled the little white room with their hum and their motion, but he was unaware of them. His arms lay across his widespread knees; his hands idly folded and refolded a sheet of notepaper.

On the paper was the heading "Social Notes." The rest of the sheet was blank. The press in the corner hadn't had its dust cover off for three weeks. Back-east editions of the *Clarion* would be a farce now, and there were too few local people left to make a county edition worth the effort of setting the type.

The square below the window was deserted except for Charlie Gates' sow rooting along the edge of the road.

Three transient wagons stood in front of the Borofens' store, and there were sparks flying from the dark interior of Charlie's blacksmith shop, but these were the only stirrings of humanity in sight. As he watched, Mel saw Will Junior on his bald-faced sorrel riding across the road toward the mill. Probably looking for someone to race with, he mused. Poor Will Junior, a whole empty town square for a playground and no one left to race with him.

His depression grew heavier. He felt angry, frustrated by the forces that were slowly pushing him toward the one thing he wanted least to do, to pick up and start all over again in another raw little town, to pry himself and Mary Pat away from the home they'd made here, to forget the picture of himself that he'd cherished all year —the founding father of Eden City, the popular and influential editor, the shaper of minds, the advocate of the better things in life. Setting aside this vision was the hardest part of all.

Focusing far down the road again, he saw Janet come out of the store and cross the road to talk to Will Junior. She appeared to be trying to get him to do something he didn't want to do. Seeing her standing there in the road, in her so-familiar gray-brown homespun with the gingham side pieces, Mel remembered how it had been when he first came here. The town had bubbled with expectations then. Optimism was in the air. The town was an unborn child, full of promise; now it was stillborn. There was no hope left in it.

Only a little more than a year ago, he mused. And Janet—big, funny Janet hanging around out at the cabin almost every day, looking at me like I held all of life's answers in my hand. A nice kid, though. Smarter than I expected. I think she was the only one in Adams County that ever read the Poet's Corner. If I didn't accomplish another thing this past year, I can't help feeling as though I did Janet some good.

He leaned forward again and looked down through the waves of heat that rose from the square. She was still standing there in the road in front of her father's store, hands on her hips, her skirt billowing in the wind.

You know, he thought, she's turning into quite a woman, with my help or without it, I'm not sure which. She doesn't hunch up her shoulders any more like she used to. And she doesn't look at me that way any more.

With an empty feeling in his stomach he realized how much he had been missing Janet's admiration these past weeks since she'd quit coming around.

When the figure in the gray-brown dress began moving up the road toward the hotel, Mel got up and left the office, not bothering to lock the door behind him. There weren't even any prowlers left in town to lock doors against. His steps echoed through the empty hotel as he went down the stairs and through the lobby.

The room was stripped of chandelier, carpet, drapes, furniture. Its bright newness was so unmarred that it could have been awaiting its first use, rather than facing abandonment. The long dining room was a barren vault without even the atmosphere of good times and memories to enliven it. A gust of wind blew ashes across the floor from the fireplace and sent a hollow sigh through the room. Mel turned away from the emptiness and went outside.

Janet saw him come out of the hotel, and for a moment she was tempted to cut across the grass to avoid him. But she squared her shoulders and met him head on.

"Hi, Janny. Where are you headed on such a hot afternoon?"

"Over to Wheelocks' to help Virgie with the packing. They're pulling out first thing in the morning, and they've got quite a bit of merchandise to get packed."

"Mind if I walk along?"

She shook her head and adjusted her stride to match his. As they passed the corner of the hotel, he touched her arm and stopped to point at the houses south of the square, in Jay Zupin's deluxe residential area.

"Have you been back there lately?" he asked.

Janet shook her head. The few houses she could see, between the store buildings, were a shambles. Windows were broken out, porches ripped off, and litter strewn thick over the neatly plotted lawns. One house had a hole in its side wall large enough for a mounted man to ride through.

"Indians have moved in," Mel said. "I spent all winter plastering those houses, and I doubt that there's a piece of plaster as big as your hand left in any of them.

I believe those Indians think we built the houses just for them to play with and have the fun of tearing down."

Janet looked away from the houses. Her voice was cool. "Oh well, I expect you'll be moving on west before too long, like the rest of them, so you won't have to look at the houses."

He turned her around and made her look at him. "Janny, that's just what I was coming to tell you. If there was any possible way the family and I could stay here and hope to make a living, we would. You know that, don't you?" He waited for her nod, then went on. "I hope you're not too, well, hurt or anything. You know you've been something special to me while I've known you."

She smiled into his eyes, a cool, level smile, and while she spoke she was exulting in the strength that kept her untouched by his words. He didn't matter any more, or at least not very much. "No, I'm not hurt, Mel. Why should I be? I didn't expect you to stay around here and publish a newspaper for the prairie chickens."

She could see in his eyes that he knew she meant it, and that he was a little deflated by her calmness. It made her feel good.

"You know what I think?" She spoke brightly and turned to continue walking toward Wheelocks'. "I think this gold rush will turn out to be a good thing for Willard's Ford in the end. There'll be other settlers later on, real settlers who'll come here to make farms and homes and to stay put. I realize you can't wait around for that to happen. You've got a family to support. But I don't mind waiting. Well"—she stopped in front of Wheelocks' store—"I'll be seeing you and Mary Pat before you leave, probably. Tell Mary Pat I'll come out and give her a hand with the packing. I'm getting pretty good at it."

She went inside and left him looking after her.

Virgie was in the large room behind the store, wrapping the family's crockery in the children's winter clothes and packing them in a large wooden crate. She worked silently, but when she raised her head toward Janet, tears were rolling steadily down her cheeks. In spite of her toothlessness Virgie had always looked young for thirty. Today she looked her age, and older.

With a minimum of conversation Janet began wrapping dishes. Once, Virgie stopped working and looked around the room, her big-veined hands hanging still inside the packing crate.

"You know what it is that I hate most, Janet? It's leaving them cupboards. Mister worked all winter on them cupboards, and you know, it really makes a place *home* when you got good solid wood cupboards with regular doors to keep your things in, instead of those awful old packing crates with curtains tacked over the fronts."

Janet looked around the room. "They sure do make the difference, all right." She ached for Virgie, as she had for every wife she'd said good-bye to this past month.

Each one of them had some symbol of permanence that she had tied her heart to, but which now must be left behind—a lilac bush, a room with plastered walls, real cupboards.

Virgie resumed working. "I just hope the Indians don't get at my cupboards. I even have dreams about it, seeing them breaking up my cupboards that Mister worked so hard on, just ripping them up for the fun of it."

"I'll try to see they don't," Janet said, knowing there was little she could do to stop them.

She stayed and worked until nearly sunset, then started home across the forsaken square. The sky had clouded during the day and was now a sheet of pearl-gray, so neutral that it drained away the little color that was left on the landscape—the tawny shade of sunburned grass, the drab tones of unpainted wooden buildings just beginning to go from new-wood gold to weathered-wood gray.

For a moment the sun, close to the horizon, broke through the clouds and turned them pink and gold. Janet slowed down and turned to walk backwards for a while, to watch the blank faces of the hotel and the other buildings turn pink in the light.

She felt good. In spite of Virgie's tears and her father's despair at the death of his town, in spite of the loss of Mel and Mary Pat, she felt good. Willard's Ford was back to just about what it was a year ago, except for all the empty new buildings that cluttered her prairie. The town's about the same, she thought, but I'm not.

She passed Charlie's blacksmith shop, and paused to look up the road toward Mel's cabin.

He hurt me, she thought, but it was my own fault. I made him up in my mind to be something he wasn't, and then I let it show. Next time I'll handle myself better.

She bent over slightly as she walked, and pulled up a milkweed stalk.

They are spreading, she mused, just like he said they would. This time next year they'll be across the river. Holding the tightly closed pod in her hand, she remembered the pain she'd felt that Mel could be so insensitive as to destroy the silver fluff, to gouge it out with his thumb just when she was feeling so akin to it. But did he really do any damage? she wondered now. Wasn't he just helping to scatter the seeds, as nature intended them to be scattered, so the plants could survive?

The pod in her hand lay unopened, showing the world only its ugly outside, and keeping the soft beauty within a secret.

"You better open up and let it out," she said aloud. "It might hurt a little, but that's what you've got to do. Am I going crazy, talking to weeds?" She laughed and, taking careful aim, threw the pod at Charlie's sign. With a sharp tearing sound, the much-mended gingham under her right arm ripped to the waist.

She started for the house at a slow lope. If my dream man *is* coming, she thought with sudden gaiety, I hope he holds off getting here till I get myself sewed up.

160